Teller of
Tales

by William J. Brooke

HarperCollins*Publishers*

With Love and Gratitude
to Leslie Kimmelman,
Joanna Cotler,
and
Susan Hill
My Appreciative, Caring, and Ruthless Editors,
Without whom my trilogy of tales would not exist.
And to
Lynne,
My Muse and My Fate

TELLER OF TALES
Copyright © 1994 by William J. Brooke
All rights reserved. No part of this book may be used or reproduced
in any manner whatsoever without written permission except in the
case of brief quotations embodied in critical articles and reviews.
Printed in the United States of America. For information address
HarperCollins Children's Books, a division of HarperCollins Publishers,
10 East 53rd Street, New York, NY 10022.

Library of Congress Cataloging-in-Publication Data
Brooke, William J.
  Teller of tales / by William J. Brooke.
      p.   cm.
  Contents: The Emperor's clothes are news — Rumpelstiltskin by any other
name — Gold in Locks — Little Well-Read Riding Hood — Teller's tale—
Tale of tellers.
  ISBN 0-06-023399-0. — ISBN 0-06-023400-8 (lib. bdg.)
  1. Fairy tales—United States.   2. Children's stories, American.   [1. Fairy
tales. 2. Short stories.]   I. Title.
PZ8.B682Te   1994   93-43421
[Fic]—dc20   CIP
                                                                    AC

Typography by Elynn Cohen
1   2   3   4   5   6   7   8   9   10
❖
First Edition

Also by William J. Brooke

A TELLING OF THE TALES
Five Stories

UNTOLD TALES

A BRUSH WITH MAGIC

Contents

The Emperor's Clothes Are News / 1

Rumpelstiltskin by Any Other Name / 47

Gold in Locks / 73

Little Well-Read Riding Hood / 103

Teller's Tale / 119

Tale of Tellers / 149

The Emperor's Clothes Are News

"Look!" shouted the nice-looking little girl. "The Emperor has no clothes!" The people gazed in astonishment, and the little girl removed everything of value from their pockets.

The more they stared, the less sure they were of what they saw. The annual birthday parade was meant to demonstrate the Emperor's closeness to his people. Close he was at the moment, but visible he was not. Almost nothing could penetrate the thick isinglass windows of the special arrowproof carriage, including light. What little could be seen was further blocked by retinues of retainers, contingents of courtiers, and gaggles of guards. All that could finally be seen of the Emperor was a large, dim, half-glimpsed shape that might just as well have been a big dog except for the bright-golden shine of his crown.

It was difficult for the good common folk to believe the Emperor would appear even dimly in public without clothes. But perhaps it was a new Court fashion. Rich folk do peculiar things. Besides, why would that nice little girl tell a lie? Now where had she gotten to? She was here just a moment ago.

"Are they appreciating me?" the Emperor whispered through the window to his Prime Minister riding beside the Imperial Carriage. "Do they look upset about the new tax?"

"Not at all," replied the Prime Minister, leaving the Emperor to guess which question he was answering. "They like to see you dressed in your best." He marveled to himself how the Emperor could make even cloth of gold look as rumpled as an old dog's blanket.

The Emperor glared out at his beloved people,

whom he did not much like. They appeared to him a sort of dim, gray fog lurking just beyond the protection of his entourage. "What are they shaking at me? Are those swords?"

"No," the Prime Minister assured him. "Those are little flags, which they wave spontaneously in your honor as per your Imperial Decree. And they are gazing at you in naked admiration."

"How very nice of them," said the Emperor nervously, giving them an uneasy wave.

"Why is he shaking his fist at us?" asked a woman in the back of the crowd.

"Has he really nothing on?" asked someone else.

A stately baker of bread shouldered his way into the front row, blocking everyone's view. Since most of them needed what he kneaded, and more than a few owed him money, they didn't dare complain. But they called out their questions to his broad back. What was the Emperor wearing? Or not wearing?

This large and vain baker reached for his gold-rimmed eyeglasses, but they weren't in their usual place. He patted all his pockets, but never thought of checking the pockets of a certain nice-looking little girl.

Giving up his search, the baker squinted seriously in the direction of the hoofbeats and announced, "I can't *see* any clothes." Of course, he couldn't even see the coach, but he knew his neighbors would expect a definitive statement from one they considered a pillar of the community.

His neighbors, in fact, considered him a pompous oaf, but outstanding bills have a way of silencing dispute. "Yes," cried one who just happened to owe the most, "he was completely naked, as our distinguished baker said. I could see, too." And others hastened to agree. "Not a stitch on!"

"Except his crown!" yelled a butcher. He was a disgruntled man who disagreed with everything so he would be considered an original thinker and a man of wit. He was considered a smart aleck, but everyone owed *him* money, too, so they laughed when they realized he was trying to make a joke.

The baker turned and glared at the butcher over the eyeglasses that he forgot he wasn't wearing. "This is not a laughing matter," he rumbled. "Our Emperor always does what is best for us, and if he chooses to wear nothing south of his crown, then he must have a serious purpose."

"Perhaps it is a symbolic gesture," agreed a threadbare preacher who hoped for a discount on his daily bread. "A symbol of sympathy for all the poor people who have nothing to wear."

The butcher laughed, after checking to be sure there were no guards within earshot. "More likely a symbolic taunt that as long as he wears his crown he can do whatever he pleases."

There were a few laughs from those who hoped for less fat on their pork chops, but they turned them into coughs at the baker's angry reply. "I won't listen to this treasonous talk," he huffed. "The parade is over. I suggest we all show our appreciation of the Emperor by going home—"

"And removing our clothes?" the butcher broke in with a nasty laugh. The crowd, sandwiched between meat and bread, looked nervously from one to the other.

The baker turned a haughty and nearsighted gaze on the butcher. "Exactly." The crowd gasped in surprise. "By removing our clothes and . . . taking a bath." The crowd laughed and applauded the baker for finding such a reassuring combination of symbolism and practicality.

"Well," the butcher crushingly retorted, "if it

gets *you* to take a bath, the Emperor will have finally done some good after all." He didn't actually
say that out loud, since he needed bread, too. But
he mumbled it under his breath and chortled and
considered himself the winner in the exchange.

The crowd dispersed, and the emptiness of their
pockets soon filled their thoughts far more than
any imperial eccentricities. That would have been
the end of it, but for a little old man who stood
mumbling and scratching his head in the street.
His pockets had been empty even before he arrived. He was upset not over something precious
lost but over something unwanted gained. "Write
what you're told!" he mumbled fiercely, and rubbed
at his temples as if the itch were deep in his brain
and would never go away.

In the main square of town, near the high walls of
the Imperial Castle, were the booths of vegetables
and fish and cloth and household goods that made
up the main marketplace. The vendors sang out
their wares and trumpeted their superiority, while
the buyers tried to shout the prices down.

A few hours after the parade, the old man came
timidly into this noise and confusion, clasping a

few sheets of paper tightly under one arm. He stood by a fishmonger's, took a deep breath, and held up his sheets. "Read the newest!" he called. "Buy my papers! Read all the newest happenings from the Emperor's Birthday Parade! All true, just as told to me! Read the newest! Buy my papers!"

The crowd paused in its ebb and flow to laugh at the old man with his hoarse, croaking song. "Newest-papers?" a man jeered. "What's a newest-paper?"

"Is it an Official Proclamation?" asked a woman. That quieted them for a moment. The Emperor loved to issue Proclamations and have them posted about town. At the drop of a hat, he would issue a decree forbidding the dropping of hats.

"Nah, look at it!" called a tall man derisively as he grabbed a paper from the old man and held it up. "No big red letters, no fancy seal, no writing so pretty you can't even read it. Just all these little, blocky, boring letters."

"I call it printing," the old man gasped, stretching on tiptoe to grab the paper back and hug it to himself. "I do it on a machine that I invented myself. My name is Teller, which I am told is the German word for plate. That's what I do, just serve up whatever is dished out. I'm a scribe, you see, and I make my living writing letters."

"And a fine living it is!" called out another man, pointing at the shabby clothes and the belt with extra notches that charted the shrinking of both the old man's income and his belly.

"There's no address on the letter," commented another man. "Who's it supposed to be to?"

The old man named Teller tried to explain over the noise and laughter. "It's not to anyone. In particular. That is, it's to *every*one, in particular. Everyone likes to get letters, and they pay to get them, so I've written a sort of letter to everyone at once telling them the amazing thing that happened."

"And you saw this amazing thing?"

"Oh, no, it's just what I was told, that's what I wrote. 'Write what you're told and you'll never be cold,' that's my motto. So I took down exactly what I heard, just like in a letter. All about the Emperor appearing with nothing on at his Birthday Parade."

"I didn't hear nothing about that," said a large woman who was buying a fish.

Teller appealed to her. "That's why you should read my . . . my 'newest-paper.' You won't hear it anywhere else. Please . . ."

"Smells fishy to me," someone said.

"It does?" the large woman asked, sniffing at her purchase. "Are you sure this is fresh?" she demanded of the fishmonger.

"Of course it's fresh!" the fishmonger replied indignantly, turning on Teller. "Here, you!" he carped. "You're bothering my customers!" He left his perch to threaten the floundering old man with a pike. "Move along now!"

"But my newest-papers!"

"I'll give you something to put in the 'newspapers'!" the fishmonger snarled. He hooked one from Teller's grasp and wrapped the lady's fish in it. "There you are, good as news."

The old man clutched his remaining papers and ran off through the market with laughter ringing cruelly in his ears.

Teller hid in an alley. He had no money left and had printed his last ten sheets of paper. This was the end of the road. But why? He was a good man. He had written what he was told. Mostly. Why should he be left out in the cold?

He put his hand into his pocket. He didn't know what he was looking for—money, crumbs of food, perhaps just a little hope.

"Nothing there," said a voice. "I already checked."

"Fine," Teller thought bitterly. "Nothing is left except that voice I have tried so hard to lose." Turning to go, he made fists and rhythmically pounded his temples as he recited, "Write what you're told and you'll never— Oh, hello!" He stopped short when he saw a nice-looking little girl standing there.

"Who are you talking to?" she asked.

Teller shook his head. "I'm sorry, you sounded like . . . well, someone I've heard before."

The little girl stood with hands on hips and watched him curiously. Her clothes were poor yet neat. You wouldn't notice her in a crowd, but when you had occasion to look at her, you realized that her short red hair and big eyes were attractive.

"Where are your parents, little girl?" he asked, nervous at her unblinking gaze. "Why aren't you playing or whatever you do?"

"Why aren't you selling your papers?" she demanded.

"You don't understand these things," he began. "You didn't see what happened—"

"I saw," she broke in. "I was busy at the back of the crowd, but I got a good look at your sales technique. I'd starve if I couldn't work a crowd better than that."

Teller looked at her in surprise. Those attractive eyes looked back calmly, not like a child's at all, or at least no child Teller knew. Of course, he didn't actually know any children. Like no child's he could imagine, then.

"If you want to sell your papers, you have to say they'll make people feel better," she went on. "Or give them some advantage or make them rich."

"But that would be lying."

"No, that would be selling. The first step is to get their attention."

"Well, that's why I made the letters bigger here at the head of the line of type, to catch your interest and make you want to read on." He held out a paper, and she looked it over dubiously.

"Can you read?" Teller asked timidly.

"When there's something worth reading," she replied. "'EMPEROR WEARS BIRTHDAY SUIT IN BIRTHDAY PARADE.' And who said this 'head-line' of yours? The 'well-placed source' you mention a bit farther on?"

Teller blushed. "Well, no. He was a baker, actually, but that didn't sound important enough, so I
made him a 'source.'"

"Well-placed?"

Teller nodded. "Front of the crowd."

She smiled. "You're less strict with the truth than
I thought. There may be hope for you yet." He
started to protest but she stopped him with "So tell
me, who said this thing about the birthday suit?"

Teller's eyes shifted away from her gaze. "Well,
no one, actually, it was . . . the voice."

"The what?"

"The voice!" he repeated. "The voice that comes
to me and whispers foolish things. If the customer
says, 'Dear Cousin Horace,' it tells me to write
'Drear Cussing Horse.' Silly things like that. So I
recite what my father taught me, 'Write what
you're told and you'll never be cold,' until the
voice goes away."

She looked at his shabby clothes. "You've never
been cold?"

"I've almost always been cold," he admitted.
"Once my father trained me, I had to leave my
family and my town because there was only
enough work for one scribe. Then, just when I

began to make a living, peace broke out and all the young men who should have been off fighting were now hanging around street corners. To keep them out of trouble, their parents set them to reading and writing. Who would hire a scribe when any convenient teenager can do the job for you? Literacy spread like the plague, and my employment sickened and dwindled.

"Then the voice spoke up with the idea for my printing press. I saw a peasant in a vineyard catch his shirt in a winepress. 'Why not ink instead of grape juice?' the voice whispered to me. I was desperate, so I paid the last of my savings for an old winepress and wood to carve into letters. It worked wonderfully, but the Guild of Imperial Scribes controls all copying of books and Official Proclamations. What did that leave? I had a press but nothing to print on it until the voice suggested these newspapers to me."

She gave a laugh and her eyes glinted. They were green, Teller noticed with pleasure.

"I like this voice of yours," she said. "He and I could make some money together, if only he didn't drag you along with him."

"The voice is a curse!" he insisted, then softened.

"Although I do like my headline. Don't you think it's clever?" He looked at her, hoping for approval, but she was back to her stern adult look. "And it makes you want to read on to get all the details."

"I don't know that I'd *want* any details about the Emperor with his clothes off. Listen, why don't you go back out there, and I'll see what I can do to improve your sales and finish my own business." She pushed him abruptly to the mouth of the alley.

Teller turned back from the open marketplace to protest, but she was gone.

"Newspapers," he whispered timidly as he walked through the market. Amid the hustle and bustle, he was quite inaudible. Halfway across the market, no one had bothered him yet. Once past the fishmonger's stall, it was just a quick step into the street that led to home and safety.

"Oh, sir! Please help me!" sobbed a loud voice.

A little girl stood in abject misery before him. It took a moment to realize it was the same little girl, she was so transformed by grief. "What's the matter?" he whispered.

"What's the matter!" she shouted. "I'll tell you!"

"Shh!" he cautioned. "People are noticing us."

"You again!" shouted the fishmonger, stepping out from his stall. "I thought I told you— "

"Please, sir," stammered Teller, "I was just leaving . . ."

" The matter," yelled the little girl, drawing the crowd's attention, "is that my mother started reading the newspaper you wrapped around her fish."

The fishmonger nodded. "And something in that piece of trash offended her."

"Oh, no," said the wide-eyed little girl. "She said it was the most interesting thing she ever read. But I had torn off some of the paper to play with, so she couldn't finish reading it. If I don't get her a new paper, she'll spank me!"

The crowd murmured in surprise. "Just over this newspaper thing?" asked the fishmonger.

"Oh, she said it was worth a great deal, that a person who didn't read it would never understand about the Emperor and the new taxes, and it would cost them money in the long run."

The crowd exchanged thoughtful looks.

"Please, sir, how much would a new paper cost?"

"Oh," Teller muttered, still trying to be inconspicuous. "I hadn't thought up any—"

"A penny!" cried the little girl. "I can't afford a

penny!" The crowd's murmurs showed they thought that too much, also. "And yet," the little girl called, "my mother said this paper is worth its weight in gold! Oh, please won't someone help me buy such a valuable newspaper with such an interesting headline and save me from a whipping?"

Teller started to give her one for free, but the little girl, in her grief, accidentally stepped rather heavily on his foot and threw him a surprisingly merry green-eyed wink, which made him hold his tongue.

"You're a very brave little lady," said a well-dressed man. "Here's a penny for your paper."

"Bless you, sir!" said the little girl. She took the penny and continued to stare at him.

After a moment's discomfort, he said, "And I suppose I'll buy one for myself." He handed Teller a penny and took a paper.

Suddenly, there was a flurry as the crowd realized all at once that they were going to be left out if they didn't hurry. Money and papers changed hands.

"Wait! I want one, too!" called the fishmonger selfishly. "Well, that's odd. Where has my purse gotten to?"

The papers were gone in a minute, and Teller looked around happily for the little girl, but she was gone, too. He hurried to the alley, enjoying the unaccustomed music of copper jingling in his pocket. She wasn't there, either. He stood awhile in the dark and emptiness, and the jingling no longer seemed so jolly. He called softly into the silence, "I would be happy to share my pennies with you," but there was no answer.

"Oh, well," he thought, "at least everyone loves my newspaper."

"I hate it!" shouted the Emperor, shaking his big, shaggy crowned head. "I really hate it!" He looked at the Prime Minister, who had stood without expression during his tantrum. "Don't I?"

The Prime Minister pursed his lips as if thinking of lemons and made a little hissing noise through his teeth. "It would certainly seem so," he agreed, judiciously.

"Good," said the Emperor. "That's what I thought I thought." He shook the paper that the Prime Minister had brought him. "Whoever is responsible shall be hanged and then beheaded and then chopped into bits and then ground into . . ."

He squinted at the silent Prime Minister. "I can do that, can't I?"

"You can," the Prime Minister allowed. "But . . ." He trailed off with a shrug of his thin shoulders.

"But what?" the Emperor asked anxiously. "Too much, you think? Leave out the 'chopping into bits' part?"

"And what of all the people who have read these 'newspapers'? This printing has great power to persuade."

The Emperor knotted his brows. "So I should execute everyone who has read this?"

The Prime Minister made his little hissing and did not answer.

"Just the reporter and his sources?" the Emperor suggested. The Prime Minister sucked his mental lemon without comment. "Just the reporter?" The Prime Minister stopped hissing and sighed. The Emperor stamped his foot. "Well, I have to execute someone, don't I?"

"Certainly, if that is your wish," the Prime Minister said. "But you might wish to turn this printing thing to your own advantage rather than silencing it. You might send for this print fellow and . . ." The Prime Minister hesitated.

"And?" the Emperor echoed.

"And talk with him."

"Talk with him? That doesn't seem nearly unpleasant enough. Could I use harsh language?"

"Your Majesty could of course do whatever he wishes. And once you had gotten all the good from him that you could and had achieved your own goals . . ."

"Then?" the Emperor prompted.

The Prime Minister wet his lips with a little dart of his tongue and smiled. "Why, then you could have him executed."

The Emperor clapped his hands in delight.

Teller was loaded with money. He no longer jingled; he clanked. It was all pennies, and his pockets were so full that he had to change his old belt for a thick rope to hold his pants up.

He had invested his profits in more paper to make extra copies, and all his extras sold as well. The day after the Parade, he produced another paper. There was nothing actually new to print, but everyone clamored for a new paper because none of them wanted to be less up-to-date than their neighbors. So Teller wrote down what everyone had said when they read the first paper and printed that as news. He headlined it: PEOPLE DEMAND NAKED TRUTH.

The fishmonger made a great point of calling him "old friend" and inviting him to stand by his stall to sell his second paper, which sold even better than the first.

"It won't be long," thought Teller as he drifted off to sleep that night, "before I'll be in demand in the finest circles. Why, I'll probably get invitations from all the best society! Think how happy I'll be then!"

"The Emperor wishes to see you," grunted the guard who hauled him from his bed.

Surprisingly, Teller was not at all pleased.

"What did you hope to gain by these scurrilous lies?" the Prime Minister inquired amiably.

"Nothing!" cried Teller. "Nothing but the telling of the truth exactly as I heard it!"

The Prime Minister smiled. "The ring of sincerity in your words is drowned out by the clank of coins in your pocket."

Teller tried to hold still, but he trembled with a sort of pneumonia, caught between the icy gaze of the Prime Minister and the hot glare of the Emperor. "It's true!" Teller gasped. "I printed what I was told, just as always! Am I to be punished for the words of others?"

"Yes!" barked the Emperor, but "Perhaps," hissed the Prime Minister, and the Emperor settled back growling upon his throne.

"You know how well loved the Emperor is among his people," the Prime Minister mused.

"Oh . . . yes," Teller agreed slowly, "I know how well loved he is." Which was not a lie, since he knew exactly how well loved the Emperor was, which was not much.

"And yet," the Prime Minister continued, "there has been great difficulty in collecting the new tax. The people object that the money will be used for the splendor of the Court and will do no good for them."

"Oh, my," Teller commented, thinking desperately and coming up with nothing. "They say that, do they? What will they say next!" He shook his head at all the things he couldn't imagine them saying.

The Prime Minister froze him with a sharp look. "It seems to me and, of course, to the Emperor, that the difficulty is a simple failure of communication. As you know, Imperial messages are conveyed to the people through Official Proclamations. Now, these are most elegantly written, but they do not seem to have the authority that your *printed* words convey. Your 'newspaper' has shown that the people will believe almost anything in print." The Prime Minister looked at him thoughtfully. "Do you see where we are leading?"

Teller didn't. He glanced at the Emperor, who didn't either but was doing his best not to show it. "You want me to put out a paper saying the other one was wrong?"

"No!" shouted the Prime Minister, and Teller buried his face in the floor. "No," repeated the Prime Minister in an icy whisper. "Don't you see, that would just make the people feel they couldn't trust what they read in your paper. You have already released the ball. You cannot take it back and roll again. However, unlike lawn bowling, in this case we have the option to change the 'spin' of the ball at any moment."

Teller raised his head tentatively. "You'd like to see some sports in the paper?"

The Prime Minister was beginning to view the

Emperor's "chopping into bits" idea in a more favorable light, but he went on in a reasonable tone of voice. "I'd merely like to see a more balanced viewpoint. You report all these speculations as to why the Emperor appeared unclothed at his parade . . ." The Emperor made a choking sound, and the Prime Minister hastened to add, ". . . which we neither confirm nor deny . . . but you quote only 'well-placed sources.'"

"Hah!" shouted the Emperor. "Now we're getting to it! Who are they? Their names!"

Teller was quaking and clanking again. He wanted to say he would be happy to point them out in the marketplace, but he couldn't tell their names because he didn't know them, but "I can't tell you!" was all he could stutter out.

"You are quite right to protect your sources," the Prime Minister agreed, ignoring the Emperor's furious looks. "If the press is to retain its power to convince, it must be free to use the truth wherever it is found, without regard to possible repercussions. For instance, were I to tell you that the reason the Emperor paraded naked (which I do not for one minute say that he did) was because the entire Treasury has been so exhausted in beginning good works for the people that the Emperor has felt it proper to sell his finest robes to continue these good works; and so, rather than appearing before his beloved people in inappropriate clothing, he prefers to come before them in the pristine innocence of babyhood: What would you do then?"

Teller stared at the Prime Minister, amazed that he had not dropped down dead from lack of breath halfway through that sentence. "I think," he said at last, "I would have to write down a record of what you said before I could be sure."

"Ah, but supposing I had spoken in confidence only, 'off the record' as it were." The Prime Minister winked at him.

"Oh," said Teller, beginning to laugh nervously, "why then I shouldn't print a word of it, of course." He winked back at the Prime Minister.

"No!" shouted the Prime Minister, clenching his hands to restrain them from punching the offensive eyeball. "No," he repeated, calmly. "You have printed many statements without naming your sources. Why would you not print my words and attribute them to a . . . well-placed source at Court?"

Teller looked from the Prime Minister to the

Emperor. "A source near the throne," he suggested tentatively.

"Exactly!" the Prime Minister said. *"Nearer the throne every day,"* he thought with a broad smile at the Emperor.

"Exactly," the Emperor repeated to show that he understood what was going on, which he didn't.

"So now you must go back to your press," the Prime Minister said, raising Teller and leading him to the door, "and put out another issue with whatever news you might wish to print."

"From whatever source I choose," Teller agreed with another ill-advised wink. He stopped at the door. "But what are these good works that have been started for the people?"

"Oh, look around," suggested the Prime Minister. "The Emperor is far too modest to speak of his projects himself, but I'm sure a bright fellow like you can find them if you hunt." With a hearty backslap, he spun Teller and shoved him through the door before he could ask any more questions.

"I'm not sure I like this," the Emperor whined when they were alone.

"But the people will, and they'll pay your tax more readily."

"So we get this fool to spread his lies *for* us instead of *against* us. . . ." The Emperor nodded, thoughtfully. "Our plan is a good one," he announced finally.

The Prime Minister bowed with humility, but his lowered eyes glittered fiercely. There was much more to this plan than the Emperor would guess until it was too late.

Teller was setting the words into type as quickly as his hands could move. "A source close to the throne has revealed that the Emperor went naked at his Birthday Parade because extensive projects for the public good . . ." He hesitated and the voice prompted, ". . . have stripped the Treasury bare." He giggled, then frowned and mumbled "never be cold," but he set the words and continued. "These public works include the following projects"—he hesitated—"for the common good"—he rubbed his hands together in thought—"of all."

He stopped. His hands were full of letters but his brain was empty. He could think of no way to make the sentence longer. That was all he had been told.

How could he write what he hadn't been told?

"Make it up," said the voice of the nice-looking little girl. "Tell them what they want to hear."

He looked around in surprise, but he was alone. "This is not good," he thought, rubbing at his temples. "My brain is already too crowded with just me and the old voice I'm used to. There's no room for another voice in here."

Yet there was something very pleasant in hearing her voice there in his mind. When he argued with his other voice, he was just arguing with himself. But the little girl's voice was completely different, and it made him feel less alone somehow.

"Make up what?" he asked, wanting to hear her again.

"New roads," said his old familiar voice.

"I wasn't asking you," he complained. "I want *her* back again."

"New roads," his voice repeated.

"All right," he sighed. "What about new roads?" Then he thought about it. Slowly, he set the words "new roads" in type. Yes, that made sense. The city roads were in terrible shape. Anyone doing good works might start by leveling the huge potholes filled with water and mud that splashed on the . . .

Clean the public walkways! All that mud the

people had to walk through . . .

Public baths for the people when they got splashed going to the market!

And a new covered market area . . .

His hands flew. He couldn't set the type as fast as the voice spoke to him.

"This is better than repeating what I'm told about the Empire!" he cried enthusiastically. "This is creating my own Empire!"

"He wants to destroy the Empire!" the Emperor howled. "Roads! Baths! Retirement plans for unaffiliated scribes! I'll have his head this time for sure!"

"For what crime?" the Prime Minister asked calmly.

"Why, lying about his Emperor, what else? I'll order a trial so no one can say my personal feelings affected the outcome. You can appear for me and swear that everything in there is lies."

The Prime Minister nodded wisely, and the Emperor nodded happily back at him. "Just so," agreed the Prime Minister. "I shall appear before the people to swear that you have no intention of using their money for public works but will use it as usual only for your personal adornment."

The Emperor's nods gradually died away. "Not a good idea?" he suggested.

"No," agreed the Prime Minister. They shook their heads gravely at each other.

"This newspaper thing complicates life confoundedly," the Emperor sulked. "I never used to have to explain anything. I'd just take their money and do what I wanted with it. And they never complained a bit."

"Not in Your Majesty's presence, but behind your back they spoke most bitterly."

The Emperor looked surprised. "They complained only when I couldn't hear? How thoughtful of them!"

The Prime Minister's eyes narrowed to slits. "No doubt. But they do more than just complain: They hide their goods, they falsify their accounts. In a word, they cheat you of what you have decreed to be rightfully yours."

"Ingrates!" the Emperor growled. "I'd like to have them all executed! I know, I know, you don't have to remind me, I can't be an Emperor without live subjects. It's just a happy little daydream of mine. Even an Emperor can have dreams."

The Prime Minister waited patiently for the Emperor to finish, then continued smoothly, "But since the news was reported of your planned public works, the new tax has doubled in its daily receipts. You will soon be richer than ever before!"

That pleased the Emperor, but a dark thought occurred to him. "As soon as I don't do any of those things, which I certainly will start not doing immediately, won't they be angry again?"

"That is why we must give them a symbol."

"A symbol?"

"For instance, who would ever believe that their hard-gotten pennies were lining the pockets of an Emperor who appeared before them *without* any pockets?"

The Emperor squinted in concentration. "So I should appear with no pockets in my robes?"

The Prime Minister shook his head. "No robes."

"Just a simple doublet and breeches?" the Emperor suggested with a gulp as comprehension began to dawn.

The Prime Minister's narrow head continued to sway from side to side, and the Emperor seemed hypnotized by it.

"Oh, my," he said in a little voice, "and I'm so susceptible to drafts."

The people were amazed and delighted and could scarcely believe it, but there it was in print: The Emperor was going to appear in another parade, this time not only without his clothes, but without his guards or his courtiers, all because the whole Treasury was going for the reported good works.

If this was true, then the Emperor was not the typical spendthrift everyone had thought him, but a good (albeit eccentric) ruler. On the other hand, if it *didn't* happen . . . there were dark murmurings of what the result might be. Everyone expressed an opinion and everyone bought a paper.

Teller was richer than he could have imagined, but he had no idea what to do with money. He bought a new coat and plenty to eat and couldn't think of anything else to spend it on.

The old simple pleasure of writing what he was told had left him. He had been contented—cold, hungry, but contented—when he didn't know there was anything else he could do. Then making up his story of the new Empire had so thrilled him that taking dictation, even from the Prime

Minister, now seemed a low and demeaning job.

For the first time in his life, Teller was wealthy, respected, and unhappy.

The night before the parade, the darkness of the city buzzed with excitement.

In the Palace, the Emperor had decided he couldn't possibly appear with nothing on. Riding in his carriage, he would be only slightly visible from the waist up anyway. He put on just a pair of breeches and admired himself in the Imperial Mirror. "There," he thought, "that will do fine." Then he looked a little closer and decided to do a few sit-ups, just to lend some tone to the Imperial Girth.

In a dark backstreet, a nice-looking little girl climbed to a low roof, where she bedded down near an open window. She could have afforded a room at an inn, but people would wonder about a little girl on her own and she chose independence over comfort. Besides, she told herself, she did not care for any company other than her own. A thought came unbidden of that poor, threadbare scribe and his offer to share his pennies. He was kind and thoughtful and . . .

She angrily interrupted her own thoughts. And weak! And easy pickings for a girl who knew her way in the street. In the darkness, she practiced the tools of her trade: the look of wide-eyed innocence, then the carefree smile, then some broken-hearted tears. All were working fine. She knew the crowd the next day would be ripe for the plucking, that she could pass unnoticed if she wished or play whatever part was needed. Her face smirked at the thought of all the fools in the world, but it relaxed slowly into a smile as she drifted off to sleep. Then her eyes began to move in dream and her face twisted and she whispered, "Don't leave me!" into the darkness.

"Are you there?" the Prime Minister hissed on the battlements of the castle. One of his personal guards stepped from the shadow with a salute. "You know what you are to do," the Prime Minister intoned, a glow seeming to come from his hooded eyes.

"Yes, your honor," the man stammered. "I am to dress in ordinary clothes and mingle with the crowd. When the carriage reaches the main market where the crowd will be thickest, I am to shout, 'The Emperor is wearing clothes!'"

"Not before he is completely encircled, you understand," the Prime Minister insisted, grabbing him and holding him against the parapet. "I want no escape for him when I reveal the truth to the people."

"Yes, sir!" the man gasped, and slipped away from the Prime Minister's coils.

The Prime Minister's tongue flicked over his thin lips in eager anticipation. "And just to be sure that my new government gets off to a good start, I'll denounce this newspaperman as a lying tool of the old regime. Then I'll issue proclamations of a new threat from abroad. With a reinforced army and new taxes, I'll create the Empire of my dreams!"

Teller sat up in the night with an idea. If he was going to spend his life printing the news, why not make it as new as possible? Why wait until after the parade to write about it? He began to imagine what "well-positioned sources" and "people in the know" would say when the Emperor appeared in the altogether.

He wrote it down. He was having fun again. He liked making up a story, even if it turned out to be true.

But what if it didn't? He was stopped by the sudden thought that the naysayers might turn out to be correct, that the Emperor might not bare all for his people.

Teller wrote that story, too, and it was even more fun. His head was filled with voices of outraged citizens threatening nonpayment of taxes and public demonstrations, hinting at even worse. It was crowded there in his mind, but he found that he enjoyed the company and he was much more capable there than he had ever been in the real world.

When he finished, Teller was pleased. He looked from one story to the other. The next day, one would prove to be truth and one fiction. Which to print?

Teller smiled. And printed both.

The first rays of the rising sun met the unblinking stare of the Prime Minister, lost in thought on the high parapet, gazing across the city like a gargoyle. Eventually, the warmth and brightness roused him and he set off for the Imperial Carriage House. Everyone had been warned to stay away from the Emperor this morning, and the Prime

Minister himself would drive the Carriage.

The Prime Minister smiled inwardly when the Emperor arrived wearing short trousers. If the Emperor had actually shown some backbone, he had been prepared to argue that a pair of pants wouldn't really make any difference. But this was easier.

The Emperor felt rather more embarrassed under the Prime Minister's calm gaze than if he had *not* worn pants. "I really should have some guards or attendants," he blustered nervously. "Who will help me? I don't even know how to open the Carriage!"

"Always pleased to be of service," the Prime Minister replied. He lowered the door, which revealed the steps and gave a nice open view of the whole interior. His smile grew even broader as he helped the Emperor into his seat.

The Emperor didn't like that thin, wide smile on that triangular face, and he was glad when it was only an indistinct blur through the isinglass. As the door closed, he let out the breath he had been holding and his stomach sagged happily over his belt.

The Prime Minister took his place and flicked

the reins. They moved out into the street.

The people had been lining up since early morning. They all wanted the best view. Not that they wanted to *see* the Emperor naked, but they wanted to see that he *was* naked.

In the street just before the main market square, the large baker arrived moments ahead of the Carriage and stationed himself in front of everyone. There was grumbling at that, but a look from the baker brought silence.

The clatter of hooves made them all crane their necks for a view. There were no guards, no courtiers, just the Prime Minister driving the Imperial Carriage. Golden filigree, angels and nymphs, elaborate carving and delicate inlays, they could see all that. But behind the isinglass, they could see only the gold of a crown atop a dim, pinkish shape.

"The Emperor is wearing clothes!" shouted a nice-looking little girl at the back of the crowd.

The Prime Minister pulled up short as he looked about furiously for the guard whose cry was both too early and strangely high-pitched.

"What's happening?" shouted the butcher. "What's he wearing?"

The crowd pushed forward against the baker's broad back.

"I'm trying to see!" he shouted, and shoved back at them.

"Listen, citizens!" the Prime Minister cried, leaping to his feet atop the Carriage. "Your Emperor has lied! He has robbed and cheated you! I have struggled for your good, but he has fought me every step of the way!"

Teller turned a corner into the street at that moment. Under his arms were two stacks of papers.

The Prime Minister ranted on at the stunned crowd. "He thought he could fool his people with new tricks, but today he comes before you dressed in his ultimate lie!"

"Down with the Emperor!" shouted the butcher. There were some shouts of agreement and a push forward.

"Prove your words!" called the baker, planting his bulk and holding the crowd. "Show us what the Emperor wears!"

The Prime Minister gave a nasty little hissing laugh. "Prepare to behold the not-so-naked truth!"

"Well, scribe," said the voice of the nice-looking little girl, "I see you've learned to play both sides of the street." Teller looked down to find her examining his two stacks of papers. "Which is it to be: topple Empires or create new ones?"

He felt a sudden sense of the possible, a *power* surging through him such as he had never known. "Oh, create, by all means," he answered, thrusting a paper into her hands.

The Prime Minister dropped to the side of the Carriage. The Emperor's big frightened eyes stared dimly out at him. "Can we go home now?" he whined pitifully. "I'm cold."

"You will soon be colder," the Prime Minister hissed, and venom filled his cold, snake eyes. "Behold your Emperor's truth!" he shouted, pulling open the door and stepping aside. The crowd gasped as they saw—

EMPEROR REVEALS ALL AT PARADE!

"Read all about it!" called the nice-looking little girl who held the newspaper strategically in front of the Emperor.

"No!" shouted the Prime Minister, slithering forward to pull the paper away.

"I believe you wanted this," the Emperor growled, bringing his crown down with a resounding clang on the Prime Minister's head and dropping him in the street.

Teller was sold out of one stack of papers within moments. The other stack he held on to, explaining that it was old news, not fit to read. The people buried their faces in their papers while the Emperor held his own copy somewhat lower until Teller closed the Carriage door.

The Emperor opened his window to whisper, "Thank goodness your paper was large enough to provide adequate coverage."

Teller smiled. "All the news that fits, I print."

The baker settled his new gold-rimmed glasses on his nose and read out loud to no one in particular: "'The Emperor appeared naked in his Carriage just as he said he would.'"

"And look there," said the preacher, leaning on tiptoe over the baker's shoulder. "Look at all the wonderful things he said he is going to do!"

The Emperor gave Teller a worried whisper. "What did I say I am going to do?"

"Read it there for yourself."

The Emperor read silently for a moment, then shouted, "Free grain for the poor! Housing! Doctors!"

"You see!" the preacher exulted. "He really did say it!"

"Quiet!" snapped the baker. "I'm trying to read."

Having read all there was to see, the crowd finally began to wander off.

"I suppose," the Emperor said, grudgingly, "I owe you a great deal, but I fear I'll end up owing even more because of you. I think you should get out of this newspaper business."

"As Your Majesty commands. Perhaps I could be in charge of printing Your Majesty's Official Proclamations."

"No. I employ a lot of scribes for that, and if you put them out of work, they'd probably start newspapers of their own." He looked at the paper he held. "I think your true talent lies in fiction. Just stay away from politics and current events. Perhaps something harmless like the old fairy tales would be best for you."

"But, Your Majesty, I don't know the old fairy tales! I never had time for such things."

"Then find a child to teach you."

"Where would I find a child? You can't just reach in your pocket and pull out a child!" Teller demonstrated this impossibility by reaching into his pocket and pulling out the hand of the nice-looking little girl.

"Er, did you drop these?" she asked, offering a fine new pair of gold-rimmed glasses. "I was just putting them back."

"Child!" barked the Emperor. "Where are your parents?"

The little girl looked around, then patted her pockets tentatively. "Haven't got any," she concluded with a sniffle.

"There you are," said the Emperor decisively. "Take her home with you, feed her up a bit, and get some stories out of her. All children know stories." When they both started to protest, the Emperor snapped, "That's a command! I shall send a guard around periodically to see that it's obeyed. I look forward to reading some of your nice stories in the near future."

A contingent of guards arrived to see what had happened, and the Emperor departed, invisible and happy.

Teller and the little girl looked at each other. He smiled timidly. She frowned.

"Well, I suppose we must do as we're told. Come to my inn, and I'll buy us some breakfast." He reached into his pocket and found it empty.

She smiled at his woebegone look and he couldn't help smiling back. Even with no money, he felt richer than before.

"Here," she said, pulling a bag of coins from somewhere and thrusting it at him. "You can hold them for now. The clanking was getting on my nerves anyway. Come on!" she called, and bounded into the crowd.

He hurried to catch up before she stole away again.

Rumpelstiltskin
by Any
Other Name

Once upon a time, there was a miller who was so proud of his beautiful daughter that he boasted she could spin straw into gold. The King, who had all the straw he wanted but not nearly enough gold, locked the girl into a chamber with a spinning wheel and great bundles of straw.

"If you value your father's life," he said, "you will spin all this straw into gold before morning." The poor girl said she could not, but the King refused to listen.

As night passed, the girl wept bitterly in her chamber. Suddenly an odd, twisted little man appeared before her. She told him her situation, and he asked what she would give him to spin the gold for her. "My necklace," she answered. The little man agreed, and in a twinkling, the wheel was working and the straw was spun into gold.

The King was so pleased the next morning that he locked the girl into a larger chamber. "If you value your *own* life," he said, "you will spin all this straw into gold before morning." Again she wept, but again the little man appeared. "My ring," she suggested, which was the last bit of jewelry she had.

The King was so delighted in the morning that he had her brought to the Royal Ballroom. She was horrified to see it stuffed with bales and mounds and heaps of straw. It was, in fact, all the straw in the kingdom. Having no one else to threaten, the King offered a bargain. "If you spin all this straw into gold before morning, I will make you my Queen."

The girl wept and the little man appeared. "I have nothing left," she told him, "but if you do this, the King says he will make me his Queen and

I can then give you what you ask."

"I will do it," said the little man, "if you will promise me your first little child when you are Queen." Since the girl could see no other hope, she reluctantly agreed.

So the King married the girl, and except for the occasional complaint about the lumpy mattresses with no fresh straw for stuffing, everyone was happy for the next year and the Queen forgot about her promise.

Then the Queen gave birth to a child, and the kingdom rejoiced. At the first public exhibition of the child, all the courtiers and commoners came to pay their respects. But suddenly the odd little man appeared and demanded the child for himself.

"Oh, please!" cried the Queen. "Do not take my child!"

The little man was moved by her tears. "I will come each morning for the next three days. If in that time you can tell me my name, you may keep the child."

The Queen sent messengers throughout the kingdom to gather all the names in the land. On the next morning, she tried Timothy, Benjamin, Jeremiah, all the ordinary names. To each he replied, "That's not my name."

On the second morning, she decided she'd nothing to lose and so tried all the insulting names she could think of: Bandy-Legs, Hunch-Back, Crook-Shanks, and even ruder ones. To each he replied, "That's not my name."

On the third morning, the Queen was frantic. But a messenger arrived at the last moment and told her of finding a little hut in the forest. A fire burned before it, and the odd little man danced around it, singing:

"Little does my lady dream,
That Rumpelstiltskin is my name."

When the little man appeared, the Queen asked if his name was John.

"No!"

"Tom?"

"No!"

"Rumpelstiltskin?"

The little man flew into such a fury that he stamped his foot right through the floor while everyone laughed that he had gone to such trouble for nothing.

"Is that the end?"

"What did you expect?" asked the nice-looking little girl. "Didn't you ever hear this story before?"

"No," said Teller. "I was too busy as a child for stories. I had to learn my trade."

"Well, that's the way I remember hearing it."

"From your mother?"

"No, I don't remember much about my mother except she was little use to me and so I ran away."

Teller was shocked. "Oh, I'm sure you don't mean that!"

"You left your family, didn't you?" she snapped back.

"Well, yes, but I had no choice."

"Well, neither had I. I never knew my father. I could stay and starve with my useless mother or make my way on my own. I chose to learn the way of the streets, and I've done all right for myself."

"Then where did you hear stories?"

A guarded look came into her eyes. "The back alleys are not safe for sleeping, so I climb up to the roof tiles to make my bed. And sometimes when I lie near an open window, I hear a mother telling tales to her children. It's annoying, but I put up with it."

Teller pictured her huddled in the shadows

outside the square of light. "Do you ever think of your mother?" he asked wistfully, feeling the stir of his own dim memories.

"No!" she snapped. "My mother left me. I waste no thoughts on her."

Teller squinted. "I thought you said it was you that left."

"Left me, left her," the girl said angrily, "what's the difference! When I lie on the hard tiles that I choose for my bed and hear the little ones being tucked in, it makes me glad that I'm not so weak and soft that I must waste my time with idle tales! I wouldn't repeat them now except the Emperor's arrangement suits me for the time being. As soon as I'm bored with you and this miserable little room, I'll be on my way again."

"But the Emperor ordered you to stay here and help me."

"Emperors don't impress me any more than scribes." To prove her point, she went over to the little pallet he had laid out in a dark corner for her, threw herself down, and made a great show of getting ready for sleep.

Teller sat at his desk, staring at the words she had dictated to him. He was not satisfied. Now that he was writing something completely made up, he found himself searching for the truth.

"Why would anyone make such a foolish boast?" Teller asked finally. "And why would the King marry her? And why would the little man want a human child? And why would he admit that she had guessed his name? She had no proof, so why not just deny it?" The questions tumbled out of his mouth now, and he tossed them all into the corner where she pretended to sleep. "And why was he dancing about in the woods, singing his name out, anyway? Would you hop about a fire, yelling 'Little does my lady dream that . . .' What is your name anyway?"

"My name's my business," was her surly response.

"But I have to call you something."

"Why?"

"So I can say, 'Ann, wake up, your breakfast is ready.' Or 'What would you like to do today, Beverly?' Or 'Clarissa, see what I brought you—'"

"More likely, 'Don't touch that, Dora!'" she broke in. "'Don't go out, Eleanor!' 'You got the story wrong, Fiona!'"

"I don't want to use your name against you," he

said quickly. "I just want to know . . . who you are. And I didn't think you got the story wrong. I'm sure that was just the way you heard it, huddled alone there on the roof tiles." He stared into the darkness where she was. "I've been inside, in the light, but I've always been just as alone as you. Isn't this much nicer, the two of us here this way?" When she didn't answer, he felt embarrassed and even wondered if she was really there at all. He went back to staring at the words.

She watched him for a while, from the darkness, wondering how two such different paths had crossed and how long before they separated again. Then she closed her eyes, willing herself to sleep.

Perhaps it was the unaccustomed luxury of blanket and fire, but sleep came quickly. With it came the dream.

"Forgive me, child!" The woman, her face pale in the darkness of the room. "I must leave you now."

"Don't leave me, Mommy!"

The silence.

The man in black steps from the shadows to close the eyes. "Your mother has left us."

"How can she leave if she's still here?"

"Nevertheless, she is gone. You must come with me now. There will be a place for you at the work-house."

The hand reaches for her, pulls her from her mother's side, into the darkness. Twisting away! Running!

And opening her eyes. Teller's hand was on her shoulder, ever so gently, and his face was full of concern. "I wasn't sure what to do. You were dreaming."

"I never dream," she snapped.

"You were making . . . little noises . . . and—"

"What's *your* name?" she demanded.

"Teller," he answered, glad to change the subject. "It's the German word for plate, I'm told. I like to think of myself like that, as a plate." He was feeling the full weight of her silence. "You know, just serving up . . . whatever is . . . dished out. . . . Well, enough of my chattering, you must be tired."

He returned to his chair. "Good night," he said, expecting no answer.

"Teller." Her voice spoke softly, a statement not a question.

"Yes."

"Then you can call me Tiler, for all the roofs I've called home. But don't ever think you have my real name."

Teller gazed at where she was, darkness within darkness. He raised his hands to his head and rubbed thoughtfully at his temples. Then he picked up his pen and went to work.

"Good night, Tiler," he whispered under his breath.

"That's not my name," said the odd little man.

"What do you mean?" the Queen asked in surprise. "Of course it is!"

"No, it's not. Where did you get such an idea?"

"One of my messengers heard you say it in front of your hut in the forest. 'Rumpelstiltskin is my name,' you said."

"Oh," said the little man with a wave of his hand. "I did say that, but he mistook my meaning. You see, in my native language Rumpelstiltskin means very unusual and interesting."

The Queen was dubious, but the little man looked open and sincere. "So you were saying, 'Little does my lady dream that very unusual and interesting is my name.'"

"Precisely," agreed the little man with a little bow.

"Rumpelstiltskin!" called the King from across the room. "Ha! You turned in answer to your name!"

For a moment, the little man looked flustered, then he protested, "No, I didn't! I thought you were calling my attention to something you saw that was very unusual."

The King squinted at him. "And interesting," he growled.

"Precisely." The little man smiled in a crooked little way, then clapped his hands together. "Well, if you've no more guesses, I'll just take the child and . . ."

"Wait!" said the King. "Let's admit that we have run out of guesses, but we still have one question that you must answer before you take our child."

"Certainly, Your Majesty, if it is within my power, I shall gladly answer."

"Oh, it's within your power and you'll answer quickly, too. What *is* your name?"

"My name?" The little man looked startled.

"Yes, your name! Quickly!"

"Uh, uh . . . Herbert!" The King and Queen

looked at each other, then back at the little man, who was making a great effort to look Herbertish.

"Herbert?" asked the King.

"Herbert," replied the little man.

"Herbert?" asked the Queen.

"Herbert," repeated the little man. "What's the matter with Herbert? You didn't guess it, and it's a perfectly ordinary name."

The King squinted at him slyly. "I heard you had a very unusual and interesting name."

The little man squirmed. "I meant perfectly ordinary hereabouts. Where I come from, Herbert is very unusual and interesting."

"Or as you say there," the Queen put in, "Rumpelstiltskin."

"Precisely," the little man agreed with an odd little smile of relief. There was silence for a moment as they all looked at each other. "Well," said the little man, taking a crooked step toward the child's crib, "if you've no more questions . . ."

The Queen turned to the King. "My lord husband," she said, "could you clear up a point for me?"

"Why, certainly my dear," he said with some surprise.

"What exactly is a name?"

"A name?" he repeated blankly. "Why, a name is what a person is called, of course."

The Queen stepped in front of the crib and looked down at the little man who hesitated before her. "I call him Rumpelstiltskin," she said. "What do you call him, Lord Chamberlain?"

"Rumpelstiltskin," replied that worthy gentleman, solemnly.

"And you, Prime Minister?"

"Rumpelstiltskin" came the response.

"And you, Royal Nurse?"

"Rumpasticksin," replied the Nurse, who was a little hard of hearing.

The little man looked about with confusion on his face. "But it doesn't matter what you call me, that is not my name!"

"What is a name, little man?" the Queen asked, taking a step toward him.

He shrank back a crooked step. "A name is given to you when you are little."

"You are little now," the Queen said with another step.

"No, no, I mean when you are young! Your name belongs to you, you own it, it cannot be taken away by someone else!"

"Then it is a matter of possession?" the Queen asked, stopping in her slow advance.

"Yes!" the little man cried happily. "Exactly! I have a legal right to my own name."

"Then it is a question of law," the Queen mused.

"Yes!" said the little man, making a bold little step past her toward the crib.

The Queen spun to block him. "And who is the highest embodiment of the law?" she demanded.

The little man shrank in upon himself and finally whispered in a tiny voice, "The King?"

"My lord husband," she intoned, turning to the King, who had followed all this with interest if little comprehension. "What do you call this man?"

The King knit his brows for a moment, then smiled broadly. "Why Rumpelstiltskin, of course!"

The Queen turned on the flabbergasted little man. "Then Rumpelstiltskin you are, by your own argument."

All the courtiers laughed as the little man sputtered and gasped. "You'll regret this! Wait and see!"

"What will you do?" the King laughed. "Spin straw into gold at me?"

The little man stamped his foot so hard it went

right through the floor. Everyone laughed the harder.

"You'd best go now," the King said between chuckles, "before I have you arrested for putting the monarchy on an insecure footing."

The little man withdrew his foot and walked with a peculiar little lope toward the door. He seemed to grow even smaller beneath the weight of laughter that was heaped onto his crooked back.

At the door, he stopped and turned. The laughter slowly died at the little look of sadness on his face. "Before I go," he said, humbly, "for the golden service I have given you . . . may I look once at the child?"

"Well . . ." the King started, feeling magnanimous.

"No!" snapped the Queen. "I won't have your ugly little face haunting her dreams for—" She broke off at a sound and looked at the crib.

The tiny babe had drawn herself up on the bars of the crib and was gazing at the little man across the room. A smile wreathed her face, and she gurgled with glee.

The Queen grabbed the child up and hugged

her close. When they looked back to the door, the little man was gone.

Some years later, there was a knock at the door of a little hut deep in the forest. The door was answered by an odd little, old little man who peered through first one eye and then the other at the figure on his doorstep. She was a nice-looking little girl in a shabby old cloak that did little to conceal the fine silks and satins beneath it.

When the little man stared but said nothing, the little girl nervously drew the cloak a little tighter about her face, which just showed more of the expensive cloth at her feet. "What's wrong with you?" she snapped. "Haven't you ever seen a wayfarer before here in your dirty old forest?"

"Never such a fair one," the old man said in a little voice.

The girl smiled in approval of the obvious truth of his reply. "I have run away from home," she announced. "I am sick to death of being pampered and waited on. From now on, I shall be the person I could never be at the Pala— at home. I shall be independent and entirely on my own." She nodded her head definitely, then gave him a hard look.

"Well, aren't you going to offer me something to eat?"

"Oh, of course! Come right in! Please forgive the humbleness of my little home."

"Oh, that's quite all right," she said airily. "I am prepared to accommodate my newly independent self to all sorts of unusual settings." She swept past him and stopped in dismay as she viewed the dirt floor, the sooty hearth, the one rude table and chair. "Humble is one thing," she said in a shocked voice, "but this is dismal!"

The little man said nothing but scooped up a bowl of carrot stew from the kettle bubbling at the hearth. He set it on the table and placed beside it a little mug of water from a rain barrel at the door.

The fragrance of the stew finally persuaded the little girl to lower herself with some uncertainty onto the crooked little chair. She looked about the table. "What's this?"

"Why, it's a spoon."

"But it's made of wood!"

The little man gave a shrug that sent his crooked little shoulders off in different directions. "I live in a forest," he explained.

She picked it up dubiously. "What if I get a splinter?"

"Oh, it's very smooth from frequent use."

That made her stop with a spoonful of stew halfway to her mouth. All sorts of questions about general hygiene were racing through her mind, but hunger finally won out. She managed to suck the entire contents of the spoon into her mouth without the least hint of a slurp.

"Needs salt."

"Yes, it does."

She looked at him hard. "Well, get me some salt."

He spread his crooked little arms. "I have none. I have almost nothing. Except wood, of course."

She grimaced, trying to imagine not having salt. Finally, she gave it up and ate the stew as it was. The little man sat on the hearthstone and watched her closely.

"Thank you, my good man," she said in a very adult voice as she reached without thinking for a napkin that wasn't there. After looking about, she dabbed at her mouth with her fingertips. "I really envy your simple life here. You must be very happy with no one to answer to."

"I'm very unhappy," he replied without emotion.

"Oh," she said, startled. "But your freedom, your independence . . ."

"Are not mine by choice. I am free only because no one wants me."

"Was there never anyone to share with you?"

His eyes feasted on the honest concern that showed in her gaze. "Almost, once, but it didn't work out."

"I am sorry," she said, and she leaned down from the chair to pat him on the arm. "But it is hard for me to understand. All of my life has been spent surrounded by people who pretend to care for me but really care only for what I am, not for *who* I am." She stopped then, realizing she might have said too much.

He smiled a crooked smile. "At the Palace," he said.

She gasped in surprise. "How did you guess?"

He nodded at the sleeve exposed from beneath her cloak. "Isn't that gold thread?"

"Yes," she replied a bit grumpily. "It's in everything I own. We have bales and bales of it around the Palace. It's no good for anything else, so Mother says we have to use it up however we can."

The little man tucked his head down into his shoulder and made a funny little laughing sound.

"You probably think," she said, peevishly, "that a bit of gold thread would solve all your problems, but it doesn't help a bit when you're unhappy."

The little man looked at her seriously. Even though his eyes did not quite match and rode at different levels on his face, still there was something very kindly in them just now. "No, I know well that gold thread doesn't solve anything at all. But why are you unhappy?"

She gave a big sigh and leaned her face on her fist. "Oh, it's just everything. Father and Mother have nothing in common. I don't know why they ever married in the first place. Father always seems to want something that she can't give him, and I always feel like it's my fault somehow. And Grandpa is this terrible old braggart who always says I can do the most amazing things that of course I can't. So when I really *do* something, it's never as great as what he said. But all the foolish people of the Court applaud anyway just because I'm a Princess.

"And they . . . oh, I don't know! They never let me be *me!* I'm a Princess, not a person. I'm this thing they own, and they only value it *because* they own it. So I ran away, to try to steal myself back from them."

The tumble of words stopped, and she gave him

a look that had nothing but little girl and loneliness in it. "Does that make any sense?"

"Yes," he said, softly. There might have been the gleam of a tear in the lower of his eyes. "But you won't find the thing you need in the forest, just as I wouldn't find the thing I need at the Court. Look around you."

She glanced at the dirt, at the shoddiness. She tried not to show her distaste, but she couldn't help it. "You were born to the Palace," he continued. "You would shrivel and die without the things you call home."

She drew herself up, and in that moment he could see the woman she would someday be. "I could live without anything. I could. Anything except my *self*, and that's what they want to take from me there at the Palace."

"No, they don't want your self. They don't even know that you have such a thing. Only you know that. And now I do, too."

"You do?"

"Yes. And I would give anything to possess it, but that is impossible. Only you can own your self and only you can give it away."

Her eyes melted in gratitude. "Thank you," she said.

He gave his head a little lopsided shake. "No, thank *you*."

She looked toward the door and sighed. "I suppose I must go back, but sometimes I feel so lost there."

He waggled a twisted finger at her and pursed up his lips. "What you need is a name."

She bit back a giggle at his attempt to look wise. "I have a name. Doesn't everyone?"

His eyes turned inward, and he looked a little sad as he said, "Not everyone." Then he shook off the mood and smiled. "A name is important. When everything else is taken away, it is the only thing that you still have. If you make up a name for your secret self, a name that no one else knows, then it can never be possessed by anyone else. And when you feel that you have been torn into little pieces and carried home by everyone you meet, you can still call your secret name and find the heart of you that no one else can take away."

Her eyes glowed as he finished, and she stared into the fire, thinking. When she came back from that place he could not go, she said, "I have it, I have my name, it's—"

"Don't tell me!" He waggled his arms and kicked up his skinny legs in mock alarm and pretended to be annoyed when she laughed at him. "I have enough to worry about without taking on the secrets of every runaway Princess who wanders by."

She hopped up in a flash and kissed him on the top of the head before he could stop her, which he would have hated to do. *"Former* runaway," she said, "thanks to the good counsel of a certain funny little man in the forest." She darted to the door and was almost through it when she turned back. "May I come to visit you now and then?"

He blushed bright red and turned to poke at the fire to hide his pleasure. "Your Highness may do whatever you wish."

She shook her head. "Not here. In this hut, I must ask permission of its ruler." She paused and looked puzzled. "I don't know your name."

His back was still turned, but one shoulder slumped even lower while the other pressed up tight against his ear. "I once had a name, but it was stolen from me."

She was too happy to catch the sadness in his voice. "I thought you said your name was all that couldn't be taken from you," she teased.

"I didn't hold it secret enough, and it was wrested from me through guile."

"Well, what *was* your name?" she demanded.

"It will sound strange to you," he answered, not wanting to say it. "It was very unusual and interesting."

"Rumpelstiltskin!" she cried.

"What!" he exclaimed, spinning to face her.

"Oh, it's just an old joke around the Palace. I never understood it, but whenever something is a little odd, they call it Rumpelstiltskin and laugh. No one would ever explain it to me."

"Herbert," he said. "My name was Herbert."

"Oh," she said, and couldn't think of anything else to say about that. She looked out into the daylight. "I suppose I should be going."

She turned back suddenly, and an idea burned in her eyes. "Would you mind if, when I come to visit, I call you . . . I mean, 'Herbert' is a perfectly nice name, but . . . Would you mind if I call you Rumpelstiltskin? You are really the most unusual and interesting person I've ever met."

A big smile grew on his face. "It would please me greatly."

She nodded to settle it. "And you must call me . . ."

"Your Highness!" he finished for her, and made a perfectly comical little bow.

"Precisely!" she said with a laugh and was gone.

Gold in
Locks

h e awoke the next morning in his chair. He still held his pen, but instead of paper it was a bowl of porridge that sat before him.

The little girl was across from him, eating a piece of fruit. His story was facedown before her on the table. "Did she read it?" he wondered, but "Where did you get breakfast?" he asked.

"Where did you get your words?" she asked.

"I'm not sure," he answered. "The voices, I suppose. I hear voices. Do you ever hear voices?"

She chewed a bit. "When people talk to me. When they don't, I don't. And all your questions about my telling of the tale, did your voices give you any answers?"

"No, perhaps not. But I thought about the questions while I wrote, so maybe it's all there somehow. In a newspaper, you must have answers, but I think a story only needs the right questions. That's why stories don't have headlines." He looked at her shyly. "Did you like it?"

"I got it at the market."

"What?"

She waved her half-eaten apple.

"Oh. How is it?" She didn't answer, just kept chewing. "Well, you don't have to pay for our food, you know. I'll take care of things."

"Don't worry, we'll work it all out in the end."

"And do you always answer questions five minutes after they're asked?"

"No," she said, thoughtfully, "sometimes I don't answer them at all."

"In other words, I should expect the unexpected."

She shrugged. "Don't expect anything. That's my system. Then you're never disappointed."

"Well, you should have more than just an apple. You need your strength."

"For what? Are you going to order me to clean your room?"

"No, no, certainly not." He looked around, surprised. "Does it need cleaning? Well, I'll do that tomorrow. Today, we're going to . . . well, do whatever it is little girls like to do."

"I don't know about 'little girls,' but I like to go out windows and across roofs and down drains and slide through crowds and make myself invisible. Care to join me?" She smiled broadly and arched her brows questioningly.

He pictured himself dangling from a drainpipe. "Perhaps I'll do the cleaning today and just have dinner ready when you get home."

He realized he had dipped his pen in the porridge and turned to reach for a spoon. "It was all right," she said behind him. When he turned back, her apple core was sitting on his story and she was gone.

"My story or your apple?" he wondered into the emptiness.

Teller meant to do the cleaning and he meant to

get the dinner, but he forgot as he read his story over and over and wondered where it had all come from. In the days ahead, she told him more stories and he asked questions and listened to voices and put words down on paper. The more he looked for the reality in the stories, the less he noticed the ordinary things around him. The girl seemed perfectly happy to do the few small tasks needed around the household as long as she was not ordered to do so. She acquired food through her own techniques and told him when to eat it. She did the only cleaning that was done, and since she was fairly unconcerned in that line, there was an accumulation of dust on everything that didn't move. This included Teller when he was under the thrall of his voices. So even as his thin features grew ever sharper, his general appearance became dustier and vaguer.

When he had five stories, he set the type for his press and printed ten copies and bound each set in a heavy piece of parchment. He wasn't sure what to do with them then, so he carried them out into the marketplace.

"Stories," he called. "Fresh stories! Come get your new stories!"

"Here," called the fishmonger, "I won't be left out this time! I'll take one of your newspapers."

"I've given up on newspapers," Teller told him and the others who quickly gathered.

"But you said 'news stories,'" the fishmonger objected.

"No, I said 'new stories,'" Teller answered. "Or, actually, old stories told new. The stories themselves are old familiar ones that everyone knows."

"Then why buy them from you," asked the fishmonger, "if we already know them?"

"Well," Teller stammered, "they're told a new way . . . and they say new things . . . "

"You mean they're brought up to date?"

"Well, no, not really. They're the same fairy tales you heard from your mother . . ."

"Fairy tales? Those are just for children!"

"I don't know. Something in them interests me. And the voices speak easiest through something we all know. When we look at a thing from only one direction, we never see all that it might be just around the corner."

The fishmonger snorted. "I think, old man, that you've gone a little around the corner yourself." The crowd laughed and went about its business.

No one wanted to buy a book of old stories that their mothers had told them without charge.

Teller finally went to see the Emperor. It took a while to gain an audience, but the memory of Teller's newspapers was still too fresh to risk offending him.

"Well, well," the Emperor exclaimed with false heartiness, "look who's here! My old friend! How are things outside the newspaper business?"

"Slow, Your Majesty," Teller replied with a great show of reluctance. "I have done my best to carry out Your Majesty's wishes, but no one wants to buy my stories. They all want me to go back to printing newspapers. Which," he added hastily, "I would of course never do!"

"Of course," the Emperor agreed with a frown.

"So I have my books of stories as Your Majesty commanded, but no one to buy them." Teller held out his little stack of books to show the truth of his statement.

The Emperor stared for a long moment, then called out, "Prime Minister!"

A chubby little man rushed in through a door and bowed repeatedly. "Your Majesty! Did I keep Your Majesty waiting? I was just taking a moment to get some food. I haven't had time to eat in three . . ." When the Emperor scowled, the little man made a quick nervous gesture. "No matter! No matter! What difference my discomfort when Your Majesty's convenience is . . ." The scowl darkened. The little man watched it in trembling silence, then threw himself into a deep bow. "Yes, Your Majesty?"

The Emperor slowly let the scowl slide from his face. He was very fond of his new Prime Minister.

"This man is trying to get people to buy copies of old stories that everyone already knows!"

"He should be ashamed of himself!" the little man exclaimed, cheeks quivering with indignation.

"But I have changed them," protested Teller, "so that they are like new stories now."

The Prime Minister cautiously glanced at the Emperor, who was careful to show nothing on his face, an expression he was particularly good at. "Well, that would of course be a mitigating circumstance."

"What!" burst out the Emperor. "That he claims to tell old stories while really telling new ones! And vice versa!"

"Fraud!" shouted the Prime Minister, trembling

with fear and indignation. "Your Majesty is right! He should be executed at once!"

The Emperor's eyes widened in mock astonishment. "But I am the one who ordered him to tell these stories. Are you suggesting that your Emperor is part of a criminal conspiracy?"

"Certainly not!" the Prime Minister gasped, dropping to his knees because he could no longer stand. He teetered for a moment, then flopped forward onto his face. "What does Your Majesty wish me to do?" he moaned into the floor.

The Emperor beamed at Teller, like a man showing off his new dog's best trick. "Why, buy his books, of course."

The Prime Minister crawled over to Teller and handed him a gold coin from his purse. He glanced at the Emperor, who looked serious, and handed over another coin. The Emperor looked thoughtful, so he started to pull out another, then simply handed over the purse.

The Emperor smiled. He really liked this Prime Minister.

Teller hurried home with the bag of gold. He took from beneath his bed the little lockbox where he kept his money. Now gold would nestle with copper in unalloyed happiness.

He set the box on the table and dropped the first coin through the slot in the top. He always enjoyed the *Clink!* of metal on metal, a pleasure derived from the long years when the coins in his pockets were poor orphans with no one to clink against.

The coin went *Clunk!* into the box.

"Clunk?" he asked himself. "That is the sound of metal and wood." He opened the lock, raised the lid, and looked in to see the gold coin in isolated splendor. Where had his pennies gone? He had not looked in since . . . since Tiler came.

Another man might have been angry to realize that he had been robbed, but Teller felt only a great sorrow. This little girl with no family had never learned better and had had to make her way alone for so long. And she had been spending at least part of the money on him, anyway, so what had he to complain of? Still, he felt he must teach her what was right.

When she came in later with his dinner, he was sitting at the table with the box before him.

"I have neglected you," he began, "and you have

fallen into bad ways." She eyed him suspiciously. "You felt it necessary to take what wasn't yours. You took from me and perhaps from others. That must stop at once. From now on, this box that contains all my money will sit here on the table and whatever you need you may take. Anything that's mine is yours, so it is now impossible to steal something that already belongs to you."

Surprise was all the little girl showed for a moment. Then she tried out wide-eyed innocence, shocked disbelief, and tearful repentance in rapid succession. When none seemed to fit the situation, she stamped her foot in anger. "Why are you doing this? I thought we got along well."

"We do," he said firmly. "I . . . like you. You are like a friend to me. But there are things that you must not do. I must try to teach you what is right, Tiler."

"Don't call me that!" she snapped angrily. "I haven't pillowed on a roof tile in weeks. Happy was I when I did! Now you must call me Tailor, because you want me to cut and stitch myself to fit your fashion!"

"It's not just my fashion," Teller spoke gently, "it's what's right."

"What's right for you! I'd rather sleep on the roof and be myself!" Quick as a wink, she threw the food down on the table and hopped over the windowsill, across the roofs and gone.

Teller stared sadly after her, then looked at the gold in the box, shiny and bright and cold. His hands went to his temples.

He looked out the window after her and felt sad. She was such a pretty little girl, he wished they could be friends.

"Papa," he said, "why does she always mess with our things and then run away?"

Papa Bear grumbled in his throat. "Humans are strange. They ignore what is offered them and take what is not. They are impossible to understand."

Mama Bear nodded. "They only know how to take things, not how to share them."

"But why does she come every day?" Baby Bear insisted. "Doesn't she know we could catch her anytime we wanted? Why does she run away?"

"You might as well ask why the sky is blue," said Papa Bear, "as ask why a human behaves strangely."

Baby Bear didn't see the point, but he was trying to be agreeable. "All right, why is the sky blue?"

Papa Bear growled and Mama Bear said, "That's enough for now, dear," and the discussion was over. But later in the day, Baby Bear had an idea, and when he was sure his parents were out of earshot, he took the tools his father kept handy for repairing the chair that the little girl broke every day and sneaked into the bedroom.

The next morning, the little girl with the beautiful golden hair awoke as usual and dressed quickly to go out.

"Are you sure you don't want some nice porridge?" asked her mother with concern. "You never have any breakfast before you go running off to do whatever you do all day."

"I hate porridge!" the little girl replied, giving her head a toss that made her curls catch the light and send it dancing around the room. It would have been a very pretty picture if her face hadn't been all twisted with disgust. "It's lumpy and bland and squishy and . . ."

"All right, dear," said her mother with a sigh. "Run along and play."

The little girl skipped happily down a path. As soon as she was out of sight, she turned off at an angle into the woods. In half an hour, she came within sight of the neat little cottage that was the bears' home. She watched impatiently until the bears went out for their usual morning stroll, then slipped in through the door.

There on the breakfast table, as usual, were three bowls. She moved quickly from one to the next. "Too hot, too cold, just right!" She ate her fill, marveling as always at this wonderful food. Its flavor was subtle, lingering just beyond what the palate could define, and the texture was fascinatingly varied. Why couldn't her mother cook like this?

When she had scraped up the very last bit of food, she moved on to the chairs. "Too hard, too soft, just right!" she announced. She liked to sit there and look at the door and imagine the knob suddenly turning and the big bear standing there and roaring. It gave her delicious goose bumps just to think of it, and she wiggled around in her chair until the seat gave way and dropped to the floor with a *Clunk!*

When she had pulled herself out of the wreck of the chair, she made a great show of yawning and stretching. Then she ran up the stairs and hopped from one bed to the next. "Too hard, too soft, just ri—" She didn't finish because the center of the bed fell in and the sides snapped up around her, and in a second there was nothing to be seen of her but one hand and one golden coil of hair sticking out the edge of a mattress sandwich.

Baby Bear couldn't wait to get back, but his parents insisted on taking their full stroll.

"Goodness, Baby Bear," said his mother. "Why are you so fidgety?"

"No reason," he said with a blush. "I just want to see the little girl is all."

"We mustn't vary the routine," Mama Bear said. "Little girls are civilized and they like things done in a certain way. If we want to see her we must do it right. It would be very upsetting to her if we arrived too soon. You'll get to see her as always, a sort of golden blur jumping out the window."

Baby Bear said nothing to that, but he was unable to enjoy the beauty of the day and kept pulling at his parents' paws. Finally, the time came to return, and they entered the neat little house by the kitchen door.

Papa Bear cleared his throat. He was very strong and very calm, but it always made him a little nervous to have the first line. "Somebody has been at my porridge," he intoned.

Before he had even quite finished, Baby Bear started saying "Somebody has been . . ." but Mama Bear gave him a look and he broke off.

After a shake of her head, Mama Bear said, "Somebody has been at *my* porridge." Papa Bear beamed at her. She had the sweetest growl he had ever heard.

"Somebody has been at my porridge and eaten it all up!" blurted Baby Bear. "Can't we skip the chairs?"

Papa Bear did not even answer but moved solemnly into the sitting room. "Somebody has sat . . ." he started, then glanced at Baby Bear with annoyance for making him forget. "Somebody has been sitting in my chair," he said very deliberately.

Mama Bear stopped Baby Bear with a look before he could say anything. "Somebody has been sitting in *my* chair," she announced.

"Somebody has been sitting in my chair and broke it all up!" Baby Bear called as he ran up the stairs.

Papa and Mama Bear followed slowly, shaking their heads.

"Somebody has been sleeping in my bed," said Papa Bear.

"Somebody has been sleeping in *my* bed," said Mama Bear.

"Somebody has been sleeping in my bed!" shouted Baby Bear. "And there she is!"

The two big bears looked automatically toward the window, but there was no one there. Then they saw the wreck of Baby Bear's bed and moved forward slowly. Mama Bear sniffed warily at the one gold curl, and Papa Bear gave the one chubby little hand a warm lick. When the fingers wiggled, Mama and Papa Bear looked at each other.

"Can I keep her?" Baby Bear asked, hopping with excitement.

It was very stuffy being trapped in the mattress, but otherwise not too uncomfortable. If she hadn't been filled with fright at the thought of the wild beasts returning, she might have gone ahead with her nap. Then she heard muffled sounds and felt something big and warm and squishy run over her hand.

By the time the two larger bears had pried her loose from the mattress, she was prepared for her fate. "All right!" she shouted. "Go ahead and eat me! But I warn you, I intend to kick and squirm and scratch all the way down, so you'd better get set for the biggest tummyache of your life!"

"Calm down!" roared Papa Bear, and the little girl went pale white at the terrible sound.

"Now, dear," interposed Mama Bear in her sweetest tones, "you'd better let me handle this." She turned to the little girl. "No one's going to eat you. There's just been a little accident . . ." Mama and Papa both glanced at Baby Bear, who looked very innocent. ". . . and as soon as you're feeling better, you can hop out the window or whatever you'd like to do." Mama and Papa Bear both smiled reassuringly, an effect that was undermined by the sharpness of their big, white teeth.

"You're not going to eat me?" asked the little girl nervously. The big bears shook their heads. The little bear seemed to be giving the idea more thought until he got a poke from his father, where-upon he gravely shook his head as well.

The little girl put her hands on her hips and stamped her foot. "Well, what kind of bears are you, anyway! Here I've been so brave all these weeks and it turns out you're just tame bears after all!"

Papa Bear scowled at that. "Mind your manners, young lady. There's nothing tame about us and we resent your remark. The fact that we choose not to eat you doesn't mean we couldn't and wouldn't if provoked enough. You have been stealing from us and breaking our things for some time, and we have let you alone only because we know you are civilized and don't know any better."

"Let me alone?" she repeated in disbelief. "Let me alone, indeed! I escaped! You chased me, and it was only through my courage and skill and ingenuity that I got away each time."

Papa Bear growled at that, but Mama Bear laid a paw on his shoulder and he said nothing, just ground his teeth together.

Baby Bear was bored with all this talking. "Can I keep her?" he asked again.

"Keep me?" the little girl echoed with wide eyes.

"No, no!" said Mama Bear. "You certainly can't keep her. She's got a home and a mother of her own she must go to."

"Then why does she leave her mother and come here every day?" asked Baby Bear, and no one answered that.

"Keep me," the little girl repeated. "Here in the depths of the dark woods with only ferocious bears for company and bear food and bear chairs and beds."

"Don't worry," Mama Bear started to say, when the little girl broke in with "Okay!"

"'Okay' what?" asked Papa Bear.

"Okay, I'll stay with you." The little girl tossed her head, which she knew made her ringlets dance and showed off her hair to its best advantage. This was what she did whenever she wanted to make her mother give in to something.

"Hooray!" shouted Baby Bear. Papa and Mama Bear shook their heads in exasperation.

The little girl pouted in a very pretty way. "If you send me home, I'll tell my father how three bears set a trap for me and he will tell all the people from the village and perhaps they will come calling at your little house." She smiled and fiddled with the hem of her dress in a very charming way.

Mama and Papa Bear looked at each other. "Well," Mama said slowly, "perhaps she could visit for a few days."

"Hooray!" shouted Baby Bear again; then his face fell. "Does that mean everyone from the village won't come calling?"

"Porridge again?"

"You used to like it," said Mama Bear.

"That was before I knew its name." The little girl

sighed. "It seemed quite wonderful when I didn't know what it was, when it was strange and forbidden. Now it's just . . ." She let it drip off her spoon in big lumps. ". . . porridge."

"What a difference a week makes," Papa Bear commented from behind his newspaper, *The Bear Truth*. He felt around for a spoon and made a stab at his porridge bowl.

"Dear," said Mama Bear, "you've got my spoon again."

"Sorry," he grumbled, giving his paper a shake. "I never noticed anybody's name on things around here before."

"And must you read at the table?" she said with a very long-suffering air. "You never used to."

"Sorry," Papa Bear repeated, folding his paper and putting it down where he could still read the headlines. "It's all this bickering that gets to me."

"We'll have a nice sit-down in our chairs after breakfast," Mama Bear said soothingly.

"I hate those chairs," said the little girl. "What's the point of sitting there when no one's liable to burst in at any moment and eat you?"

"It helps us digest our food," Mama Bear replied with a tone of patience wearing thin.

"I think mine's already digested," grumbled Baby Bear, making the porridge drip from his spoon as the little girl had done.

"Baby Bear!" exclaimed Mama Bear with her eyes wide. "Wherever did you learn to say such things!" All three bears looked at the little girl.

"And that bed you made for me," she went on, ignoring their look. "I can't sleep a wink in it. If I don't die of boredom or malnutrition, I'll probably die of sleeplessness."

"No," said Papa Bear, and there was suddenly a thunder in his voice and a glint in his eye. "You're not going to die of any of those. I thought we might be a good influence on you, but just the opposite has happened. We are becoming more and more civilized. We've learned to want what we don't have and not to share what we do have and to cut ourselves off from each other. A few more days and we'll be fit to join an Emperor's Court."

"Don't get all excited," said Mama Bear, patting his paw.

"But I am excited! I know how to put things right again! We just need a change in our diet!"

"Well, I'll second that motion," the little girl said, shoving her bowl away from her.

"We need more"—Papa Bear put his big, hairy face very close to the little girl's—"red meat."

She gulped nervously, then played with a golden curl to make herself irresistible. "Beef?" she asked with a little laugh.

Papa Bear shook his head and smiled at her. "No, dear," he said.

"Deer?" she echoed, hopefully.

"That's right." He nodded. "Come here . . . dear." He stood up and suddenly looked much bigger than he had before. She hopped to her feet and backed away from him. "You have shown that you have no manners. Let us see if you have any taste!" Grabbing up a spoon, he lumbered toward her, paws outstretched.

The little girl leaped through the kitchen window and disappeared into the woods.

Mama Bear looked at her husband in shock. "Papa Bear!" she exclaimed. "You wouldn't eat a guest, would you?"

Papa Bear grinned like a very large, ferocious sheep. "It was time for her to go," he said. When his wife continued to glare at him, he added, "What was I going to do with a spoon anyway?"

"Well . . ." said Mama Bear, still not quite approving.

"Were you really going to eat her, Dad?" asked Baby Bear, his eyes wide with excitement.

Papa Bear looked at Mama Bear, who gave him a meaningful look. "Of course not," he said, innocently. But when Mama Bear went to get more porridge, he winked and made terrible ripping motions with his paws, gnashing his teeth in a silent snarl.

Baby Bear looked at him with new respect and admiration and made no more complaints about his porridge. "She was so pretty," he said. "I am sorry we'll never see her again."

Mama and Papa Bear looked at each other.

"Mother! Mother! I'm home!"

"Oh, thank goodness!" she cried. "We were so worried!" And she kissed the little girl again and again and wept so sweetly that the little girl wondered what had ever possessed her to wander from home.

"I'm hungry," said the little girl, making a very sad little face that caused her mother to kiss her even more.

"Oh, dear, all I've got in the house is some porridge."

"Oh, Mother, your porridge is the best in the

world! Please let me have some right now!"

The little girl ate her porridge all down and kept talking about how wonderful it was, although she had to admit that the last bite did not taste as good as the first had.

When her mother asked where she had been, she told about the three bears in the little cottage in the woods. Her mother was horrified and wanted to run and tell her husband so the men of the village would do something about it, but the little girl said that it was probably her fault. She told how she had stolen through the door when the bears were out and how the bears had been very nice and had grown almost civilized under her good influence.

Her mother was finally convinced that the bears should be left alone, but she made her daughter promise never to set foot through the door of the bears' cottage again. The little girl promised heartily and she never, ever broke that promise, either.

After all, it was much more fun to climb in through the window.

She was sitting by the window when he opened his

eyes and stretched. He shifted in his hard chair and reached for the bowl of porridge.

"Have you already eaten?" he asked. She didn't respond, and he suddenly noticed the pile of pages beside her on the windowsill. "Did you read my story?" he asked hopefully.

"Yes," she said, and his heart raced with excitement. But then she continued with an innocent half smile, "I ate at the marketplace. I only came back to tell you that I'm leaving. I'm bored with the arrangement, so I'm taking off, that's all I came back for."

"And to make my breakfast."

She shrugged. "You can starve to death after I'm gone, that's your affair."

"I'm sorry you're going."

She waited for more, but he watched her in silence. "Now, don't start threatening me," she said, "with Emperors and Guards and such. You can't change my mind."

He shook his head gently. "I'm sorry you're going."

She chewed on her lip for a while, then stared out the window. As casually as possible, she said, "Where's the money box?" She waved a hand at the table, which was empty of all save the bowl of porridge.

Teller looked very serious. "I changed my mind. I've hidden the money box away where no one can find it."

"What?"

"I hid it away during the night. I decided that what's mine is mine. And I'll do what I must to keep what's mine."

"You don't trust me!" the little girl wailed, tears bursting from her eyes.

"I trust you to be yourself," Teller said.

She sniffed once or twice, then hopped out the window. Framed against the blue of the sky, she pulled a gold coin from her pocket and flipped it high and glittering in the light of the young sun. "You should find a better hiding place than under the loose board in your closet," she called with a laugh.

Teller replied with a small smile, "You should learn to make less noise when a poor, helpless old man is sound asleep."

She looked at him curiously. He closed his eyes a moment and made a gentle snoring sound. She threw back her head and laughed, her hair red-gold in the early-morning light. Then she spun and was gone.

Teller sat alone, happy in his room, which, although empty, overflowed with anticipation and possibility.

Little
Well-Read
Riding Hood

---

everal years passed in that way they
have of seeming to crawl unbearably
slowly until you look around and find
them gone without a trace.
Teller grew feebler, and so he let the little girl
handle all his contacts with the outer world, including the delivery of the books. Every month or
so, a new set of stories would be printed and
bound and delivered to the Prime Minister. A
purse of gold would be brought back to Teller,
who would place it secretly in the money box,

where it would never be heard from again.

Teller did not miss the outside world very much. His voices kept him busy, and when they were quiet, he would ask idle questions of the little girl, who would ignore them and talk about whatever she wanted to talk about. This was very satisfactory to him.

"Do you ever hear voices?" he would ask now and again, as if he had never asked before. "It would be lovely if you heard voices, too."

"Why?" she'd ask, when she bothered to answer at all. "So that yours will have someone to talk to after we're both carted off to the loony bin?"

He shrugged. "It's just a thought I have now and then."

Of all the voices that spoke to him, hers was his favorite, and not just because it was the only real one. She had lived the life he had never dared, had experienced the feelings he had never allowed himself. If you write only what you're told, you'll find very little adventure. And he thought that perhaps she liked him because he took her seriously and never treated her like a child. But of course she never said anything, and he knew he could be completely wrong about what she thought.

It did make him laugh that, after all these years, his only friend was a little girl who took everything he owned and doled out just enough to keep him fed and clothed, treated him disrespectfully, and came and went as she pleased.

Now and again, when Teller had done something unexpectedly nice or engagingly silly, she felt the urge to give him a hug or just a gentle touch, but something inside held her back and made her angry with herself for the weakness she had almost yielded to. And, now and again, Teller wanted to ask about her life, her feelings, to really *talk* to her, but he was afraid it might drive her away. So he talked to her only in his stories. And whether she read them he could never be certain.

"You know," he pondered one day, trying to draw her out, "I wonder who reads my stories."

She shrugged. "I know one person who reads your stories."

"You do?" he asked. He was surprised to get a relatively direct answer and excited to be so near the truth. "And did . . . that 'person' find any merit in them?"

"Yes," she allowed, offhandedly. "That 'person'

thought they were amusing and well written and much better than the old stories." Teller blushed with pleasure and surprise. "And wondered where you got your ideas."

"I've often told you," Teller said, happy to tell again. "My voices. At least I think of them as voices. They are ideas and thoughts that come to me, and it is easier to hear them as voices than to think of them some other way."

"Who are these voices?"

"Some are people I've known, my parents or people I've met, but many are strangers. Many are the people in the stories who insist on speaking for themselves. And some have never been but may be someday. There is one with a strange accent who says his name is Pecos Bill and that he will invent the lariat and the branding iron and ride the tornado."

"The lariat," she said, nodding. "That's one of those . . ."

He laughed and shrugged. "I don't know what it is either. Or the other stuff. No one does. But I could write his stories," he said hopefully, "if you'd be interested in reading them."

She shrugged. "It's not up to me. You should ask the person who actually reads your stories."

"Isn't that you?"

"And I wouldn't pay too much mind," she went on, "to his high opinion of your stories, since he's so stupid he has to ask me what the long words mean."

"'He'?"

"That's right. He lives at the Court and he found the dark, little closet where all your books are put to be out of everyone's way. He only read them because he thought he wasn't supposed to. He likes them because he enjoys seeing the old stories turned inside out. He is very disrespectful." She shook her head disapprovingly at the thought of being disrespectful.

Teller was gasping, "But . . . but . . ." His mind raced and his mouth lagged far behind. "My stories are not disrespectful! They're different, it's true, but they're meant to illuminate the originals, not to corrupt them. When you read the stories with him . . ."

"I didn't say I read them. I just help him with some of the show-off words."

"And who is he, anyway, and how did you meet him and . . . What show-off words?"

"Does it bother you," she asked, ignoring his sputtering, "that all your work just goes into a closet to be read by one stupid boy who misses the whole point?" She gazed at him with seemingly sincere interest.

"Yes!" he blurted, then stopped and thought. "No," he said then, feeling his way through his thoughts. He spoke with unusual resolution, and she listened attentively. "It doesn't bother me. Writing isn't about being read. When the words leave me, the writing is over. It looks nice, printed and bound, but then it's about reading and that's entirely different. No, the pleasure is in asking 'What if?' and following wherever the questions lead you. And if there were one true secret reader to carry on for me . . ." His voice trembled, and he gazed intensely into her eyes while his hands rubbed at his temples. ". . . Who would hear my voices and ask her own questions—"

"I met him on my way once to the Prime Minister's," she broke in, tearing her eyes away and trying to chatter casually. "He saw me bringing the books and asked if I wrote them. I said, 'Well, yes, they're my stories,' which is not a lie since I tell them to you and then you put them down with a few changes. He is a nice-looking boy, but rather immature even if he is about my age."

"What age is that?" Teller found himself wondering. Then he shook his head and insisted, "This is not good, the Court is not safe. Why did I ever let you go there? It's a very dangerous world for those like us who don't know their way around. I don't think you should see this boy anymore."

She snapped back angrily, "Perhaps what we have is enough for you, but it is not enough for me! The Court seems a fine place, and someday I will find my true home there." She gestured wildly around her. "You think this is enough for me?"

His mouth hung open and his eyes were wide. "What are you staring at?" she demanded.

"You're not a little girl anymore," he stammered out. "I never noticed. I'm sorry, Tailor."

"Don't call me that!" she burst out. "You just want me to be your slave! Call me 'Toiler'!" With a sound that might have been the start of a sob, she rushed out the door.

Teller stared thoughtfully after her. It had been a long time since she had used the window. She wasn't a woman yet, but she wasn't a little girl anymore.

And, it struck like a thunderbolt, she wasn't nice-looking anymore.

She was beautiful.

— ❖ —

She walked away quickly, glad to be out of the house. She scarcely noticed the weight of her bundle as her annoyance made her walk ever faster. Irritation can be quite invigorating.

"Danger, indeed!" she grumbled to herself. "When I need advice, I'll . . . Well, I certainly won't ask for it. I'll give it to myself, that's what I'll do! Things are only dangerous if you don't know what you're doing."

So saying, she pulled her scarlet hood closer about her and rushed on. She ignored her mother's warning to stay on the path that skirted the woods to reach her grandmother's house, but hurried into the deepest, darkest part of the forest.

As her irritation began to fade, she noticed her surroundings more and started looking for some landmark. Her steps slowed as she saw nothing but forest. She should have come to a stream or a ridge that would give her a rough direction, but there was nothing except leaf and bark. Even the sun did not reach into these deep glades. Each step gave a different view down leafy colonnades, but none showed her a way out. She stopped and listened to the sound-filled silence of the deep wood, and her heart beat now with excitement rather than annoyance, and she felt the first wispy tingle of fear.

"Hello!" she called. "Can anyone hear me?" The silence seemed offended at her intrusion. It was like shouting in a church.

"Hello!" she called again. Was that the snap of a twig? She looked about, hoping to see someone, afraid to see some*thing*. "Is anybody . . ." she started to yell.

"Quiet!" came a bark from a dark thicket. A shaggy, doglike head suddenly appeared, its savage teeth bared and dripping. "Who dares disturb my rest?" snarled the wolf.

After jumping a bit at this sudden appearance, the little girl said with a laugh, "Oh, it's just a wolf!" She was quite happy to see him. Nothing is as bad in person as it is in imagination.

"'Just a wolf!'" repeated the wolf scornfully. "Look at me! See what big eyes I have!"

The little girl peered with interest into his eyes, which blazed like coals. "The better to see me with," she said. "And yet, in spite of their size, they are actually rather weak and unable to distinguish colors." She smiled benignly at him.

"Where did you hear that?" asked the indignant wolf.

"I read it in a book about the wildlife of the forest."

"Well, even if it's true," grumbled the wolf, "look what big ears I have!"

She looked with interest at his large ears, which pointed toward her with the hair all standing on end. "Yes, they're more useful than your eyes but still far inferior to your primary sensory organ, the olfactory, which you scarcely need to point out is also quite large."

The wolf was rather sensitive about the size of his nose, so he avoided the subject by baring his teeth in a snarl. "See what big teeth I have!"

"Yes," agreed the girl. "It's fortunate for me that you eat only rodents and small mammals when you hunt alone or deer when you join in a pack."

"Oh, you think so?" sneered the wolf.

"Yes, there are absolutely no reliable reports of wolf attacks on humans."

"None?" asked the wolf in surprise.

"None," she said definitely.

"Well, there's always a first time."

She smiled at him in a pitying sort of way, and his eyes shifted this way and that beneath her gaze. "You're lucky I'm in a good mood today. Otherwise you would pay dearly for interrupting my nap. What's in the basket?" he asked, to change the subject.

"Some very excellent cookies I am bringing to my grandmother."

The wolf's eyes widened. His nose twitched and his ears pointed with interest. "Cookies? Did you bake them?"

The little girl pursed her lips with annoyance and looked here and there before she answered. "Well, the idea for baking them was mine and I specified the kind of cookie to be baked. But my mother was the one who actually carried out my instructions."

"What kind of cookies?" the wolf asked, his lip curling back to show a bit of shiny tooth.

"Sugar cookies," she answered. "But Mother put in a lot of stuff on her own that probably ruined them. Nuts and gumdrops and raisins, so they're scarcely what I told her to make at all."

"Sugar cookies," mused the wolf. "With nuts and gumdrops and raisins." He was beginning to drool, and his eyes were glazed as he stepped toward her.

She hastily backed away. "The book mentioned nothing about baked goods in a wolf's diet," she said accusingly.

"Even in a pack it's hard to find a good sugar

cookie in the woods," the wolf said. "Most of the time." He stepped forward abruptly.

The girl turned and ran into the forest. The wolf leaped after her but got only the red cloak, which caught in his teeth. By the time he could disentangle himself, she was gone.

The wolf glared after her in irritation, then had a thought. He slipped his head through the neck of the hood and raced off into the depths of the woods, where he knew all the shortcuts.

The little girl ran and ran and finally found the path. She didn't vary a hair's breadth from it as she hurried to her grandmother's. It took a while to get there, and the longer it took, the sillier she felt that she had been afraid of the wolf. The book had been quite specific about that. She decided it was all her mother's foolish talk about danger in the woods that had made her nervous. She resolved to think no more about it, and yet she still walked rather faster than usual, and when she came to her grandmother's cottage, she pounded rather harder than she intended on the door.

"Grandma!" she called in a voice she meant to be calm, but it shook in a most exasperating way. "Grandma! Please let me in!"

"It's open, dear," came a muffled reply. "Come on in."

The girl thought this odd, since her grandmother was not as well read as she and therefore worried about the beasts of the forest. But she lifted the latch and walked in.

"Why is it so dark in here?" she asked.

"Oh, I put out the lights," came the voice from the bed, "because I am not feeling well."

"Yes," agreed the girl. "You sound very hoarse. Well, you must cheer up because I have brought you some excellent sugar cookies."

"Did you bake them yourself, dear?" the voice inquired in a surprisingly sly tone for her sweet old grandmother.

"Practically," she said, walking toward the bed.

"Then I'm sure I shall love them," came the gruff voice from the nightgowned figure beneath the covers.

As her eyes adjusted to the dimness, the little girl was surprised. "Why, Grandma, what big eyes you have!"

"All the better to hear you with," said the figure, which was apparently too intent on the basket to pay much attention to what was being said. "Come closer."

"And, Grandma, what a big—"

"If you're going to mention my nose," broke in the figure, "it is swollen from being blown so much, and it's not polite to call attention to it. Come closer."

The little girl arrived at the bedside and bent closer. "Why, Grandma, what big teeth you have!"

"All the better," shouted the wolf, throwing off the bedclothes and leaping toward her, "to eat sugar cookies with!"

She jumped back in horror as he thrust his hairy snout into the basket and literally wolfed down the cookies.

Just at that moment, the door was thrown open and Grandmother rushed in with a woodsman. With one blow of his axe, he chopped the wolf wide open to reveal all the sugar cookies, but of course they were not in any condition that anyone would want to eat.

"Thank goodness you're all right!" said Grandmother. "That wolf tricked me with your hood into letting him in. I thought he'd eaten you!"

"Don't be silly," said the girl. "Wolves don't eat people. It says so in my book."

"Perhaps," said Grandmother, "but are you sure it says so in his?"

Teller's
Tale

"So this is the old man. Old Mr. Plate himself."

"Quiet, you'll wake him!"

Teller opened his eyes. Peering at him from inches away was the broad, hearty face of a young man. Teller shrank back as far into his pillow as he could.

"Can he talk," the young man tossed over his shoulder, "or does he just write?"

"Of course he can talk," she said, pulling him away from Teller's bedside. The young man laughed and hopped up to sit on the edge of the table. He tried to pull her up beside him, but she drew away and smoothed out her dress before she turned back to Teller.

Her eyes shifted about the room. "This is my friend I was telling you about," she said. "Once. A year or two ago. His name is Valorian."

Teller looked at her in wonderment. She had become a woman, a beautiful woman. How did he keep missing these things?

"I am pleased to meet you," Teller said slowly. Valorian nodded his head and smiled as if to say, "Well, naturally you would be!"

"I am glad," Teller continued, "that you brought him to meet me. That was a very polite thing to do, Toiler."

She blushed and for a moment the young man watched the color mount in her cheeks as if she were a pet performing a trick he had taught it. Then he frowned. "'Toiler'? What on earth does that mean?"

Eyes down, she said nothing. Teller hastened to cover her embarrassment. "I don't know her name. Toiler is the name she asked me to call her by."

The young man laughed long at that, a loud,

hearty, irresistible laugh that irritated Teller immensely. Slapping his thighs, Valorian rolled back on the table, paying no heed as Teller's bowl and spoon and pen and paper tumbled to the floor. The young woman hurried to pick them up, but there was no place else to put them. Valorian laughed himself out, then regarded her curiously. "Toiler, eh? A good name for her. Perhaps I shall call her that myself."

"Do you know her real name?" Teller asked, feeling a little stab of jealousy.

The young man shrugged. "It's not important. I call her what amuses me. Rag-Muffin or Jill-o'-the-Wisp or Willie-Nillie. She answers to whatever suits me."

He smiled at her and she said nothing, but Teller's heart sprang back up because he knew that all Valorian's talk just meant he didn't know her name either.

"Come here, Toiler-Moiler," the young man said with his mouth scrunched up so it sounded like a baby talking. "Sit by Vally-Wally here." She stood in silence. Teller smiled as he imagined her reaction if *he* had ever tried baby talk on her.

"Come here!" the young man said in an irritated

voice that sounded much more natural to him. She sat on the edge of the table. He took Teller's things from her hands and dropped them casually on the floor. "You have company. You must stop flitting about and entertain me properly." He stopped and bent to pick up some of the pages that had scattered. "What's this? A new story?"

She looked at Teller, who said quickly, "Oh, it's not finished. It's just a bit of something. You wouldn't be interested."

"That's for me to say, not you, old man. Now, here's 'Once upon a time' and down here's 'The End.' That sounds like a whole story to me."

"Yes, but it's not—"

"Be quiet!" the young man snapped. Teller was still. At Court, he knew, good manners were a defense against the power of others; the weaker your position, the more courteous and deferential you must be. To be this rude by nature, the young man must hold a high position.

"You will read me your story."

Teller started to demur, to explain that his voice was weak, but he realized the young man wasn't speaking to him. "Not now," she said. "My voice is tired. Come, you've seen where I live, now let's go!" Teller was pleased that she was embarrassed to claim authorship in front of him.

"I'm not yet ready to go. Your voice was strong enough to dictate it for the old man to write down. You've often told me you must read it over before he sets it in print to be sure he hasn't made mistakes. Well, you can read it to me and I will help you."

Her cheeks burned and she stared at the floor.

Teller spoke softly. "My handwriting is not what it once was. Sometimes it's hard to make out someone else's writing, even when the words are your own." She flicked a defiant, spirited look at him that pleased him far more than any look of gratitude could have. This was still the girl he had known. What little he had known her.

"Well, then," suggested Valorian, "just tell it to me in your own words, Tilly-Toiler, and I'll follow along to see how well you remember it."

Her head snapped up and she gave him the look a deer wears in the moment it hears the twang of the bowstring. Before she could speak, Teller said, "But wouldn't *you* care to read it aloud for us?" Valorian gave him a frown, but Teller hurried on. "She has often told me of how you read the stories

and what a grasp you have of their fine points."
She almost giggled at that while Valorian looked
dubious. "And, of course, what a fine speaking
voice you have."

The young man thought a moment, then smiled.
"Yes, that will do very nicely. The creator of the
story . . ." He bowed condescendingly to her. "The
rude mechanic who transcribes it . . ." He gave
Teller a little wave. "And the interpreter who
brings it to full life!" He slapped himself on the
chest.

"Exactly!" proclaimed Teller with enthusiasm,
beaming at the beautiful young woman's apologetic
look and the handsome young man's arrogant one.

Valorian arranged himself in the middle of the
floor and began to declaim. His gestures were wild
and inappropriate and he would make up any pro-
nunciation he didn't know, all the while glaring at
his audience as if daring them to correct him.
They listened in silence.

ONCE UPON A TIME, *there was a gentleman whose
wife died, leaving him alone with his pretty little daughter. He
married again, hoping to gain a good mother for the girl as
well as a good wife, but he died himself soon after. The step-*

*mother inherited the house, the grounds, the fortune, and the
daughter, and she loved them all exceeding well with just one
exception, which was not the fortune, the grounds, or the
house.*

"I know this story," Valorian said, interrupting
himself and taking the opportunity to catch a
breath. His oratorical style tended to overlook
commas and periods and to run entire paragraphs
into single sentences. This encouraged the lis-
tener's imagination, since you had to picture not
only characters and action but punctuation as well.

"Yes," the young woman agreed, watching Teller
cautiously, "it does seem familiar."

*The little girl was made to do all the work for her stepmother
and to sleep at the kitchen hearth among the remains of the
fire. Her name was Etta, but she was called Emberetta, and
her only friend was a dog.*

Valorian blinked and moved his lips as he read over
the last sentence to himself. "That's not right! Her
name was Cinderella and the birds were her
friends. Or was it the mice? Certainly not a dog!"

"You know the stories are never quite what

you've heard before," said the young woman.

"Yes, I know, but this doesn't make me laugh. I mean, what's clever about having a different name or having dogs instead of birds? I have dogs myself."

"You're right," put in Teller. "There must be very little clever, then, about having dogs."

Valorian nodded, then hesitated, unsure how to take that.

The young woman looked crossly at Teller, who put on his innocent-old-man face and gestured eagerly for Valorian to continue.

She found the dog in the woods beyond the garden when it was but a puppy. She named him Bilbo and kept him in a toolshed, where her stepmother would not see him.

The puppy was lively and bright-eyed and every step was an adventure, for his big ears were always getting caught under his big paws and spilling him into a tangle of black and brown and white and pink tongue a-lolling. He would just get his various parts all sorted into proper order when another step would tumble him all over again.

Etta would slip away to Bilbo whenever she could. She loved to watch him and to play with him and to care for him. The only thing she feared was that her stepmother would find him and take him away. Or worse.

So she had to train him to be silent. This meant giving him a little smack on the tail whenever he made a whimper or a whine or the first hint of a baby bark. This smack, which seemed a terrible blow to her, was in fact scarcely enough for him to feel, but it did make him look at her with question in his eyes. "Bad," she would say, "bad dog!" He had no idea what this meant, but he would concentrate very hard, squinting his eyes and arching his back. She had no idea this was how dogs paid attention, and her heart would break at the way his tail slumped. All the toil and unkindness her stepmother inflicted upon her could not make her cry, but those big brown eyes could bring the tears to her own in a moment. She would open her arms and he would bound forward to lick the tears from her face, knowing he was forgiven for he knew not what.

Now Bilbo, it must be admitted, was not the brightest of animals, but he loved her exceedingly. He scarcely noticed her smack on his tail, for it was never more than a pat, really, but he did notice that whenever he made a noise, she would burst into tears. This upset him, even though the tears were wonderfully salty on his tongue. So he gradually stopped making any sounds and her training worked in ways she couldn't have imagined.

She also trained him to sit up, play dead, roll over, and

offer his paw to shake. She would say "Sit up!" and he would execute a perfect rollover. She would say "Shake!" and he would collapse in an astonishing simulation of lifelessness. He took any short exclamation from her to mean "Do a trick!" and he would perform whichever seemed to him most appropriate at the moment. For her part, she was so delighted with whatever he did that she preferred to believe that she had just given the wrong command and that he was perfectly trained and obedient.

So they spent their time together in total misunderstanding and harmony.

Food was always a problem, as Etta had only the meager allowance that her stepmother gave her, but she happily shared it with Bilbo, who would wolf it down in a moment and lick her face with pleasure. But as he grew bigger and then bigger again, his appetite grew even faster. He would gulp down his portion and look about for the rest of it. Etta gave him more and more of her share until she was living on mere crumbs. Still it was not enough, and she couldn't bear to see him hungry. He would look at her and she would say "No more!" and he would roll over and then he would look at her again.

She began to sneak extra food for Bilbo from her stepmother's pantry. In her misery, Etta thought of this as stealing, but in truth the food was paid for by her father's money, which had been meant for her, and so she was only stealing what was hers by right. She ate none of it herself but gave it all to the dog.

"Legally," put in Valorian, "if the father didn't specify otherwise in his will, the money and therefore the food actually belonged to the stepmother and so it *was* stealing." He looked from the old man's intent but vacant face to the young woman's, which seemed angry, although she was looking at the old man, not at him. "Of course," he went on, "in a story we must make allowance for sentimentality. It is, however, important not to confuse that with real life." He waited, watching her, until she let the fire go out of her eyes and turned to give him a little nod of agreement. Having made his point, he cleared his throat and got back to the story.

Then one day when Etta was commanding "Beg!" and Bilbo was executing a perfect series of back flips, the door of the shed suddenly opened. "So!" hissed her stepmother. "This is where my food had been going to! You're a thief as well as a liar!"

Bilbo gave a few tentative tail wags, but then he saw that

Etta was frozen in terror. Instinct rose up in him. He bared his teeth and the hair stood up on his neck. It took all of Etta's good training for him to swallow the growl in his throat.

The stepmother grabbed up an old riding whip. "I'll show you how we deal with liars and thieves!" The stiff leather whistled through the air, and Etta closed her eyes to receive the blow. But it never landed.

"Vicious dog!" Etta opened her eyes to see the door standing open and her stepmother fleeing down the road, calling for help. Bilbo quietly laid the two pieces of the whip at Etta's feet. She had never before noticed the great strength in his jaws.

"Run!" she cried, breaking out of her immobility. Bilbo rolled over, glad to see her once more in control. "No, no! Run! She'll get help from the village. They'll believe her. They'll bring weapons to hurt you. You must run!"

Bilbo couldn't understand why she was so upset. He did all his tricks especially well, but she never smiled. She shoved him out into the yard and he stood there uneasily. He had not been outside since she had taken him into the shed, and it felt strange.

She picked up a rock and he watched curiously to see what she would do with it. She threw it at him, but she missed. "Go!" she cried. He took the rock up carefully in his teeth and dropped it at her feet, wagging his tail happily at this new trick, which he was sure would please her.

She grabbed up the rock and threw it hard against his back. It hurt! He yelped in surprise and pain, then cut it short. The tears in her eyes hurt him more.

"Go!" she yelled, and "Go!" and threw rock after rock. He made no more sound but let his ears and tail droop as he took the blows and tried to understand. Then he turned and moved slowly into the forest.

"Go" was the first human word he truly comprehended and it filled him with pain.

In the forest, Bilbo wandered sad and hungry for several days. There were many small animals that might have satisfied his craving, but he knew nothing of hunting and so would merely try to play with them. When they disappeared up trees or down holes, he would be left as lonely as before.

Then one day he heard a great barking that aroused memories within him. He hurried toward the sound and was suddenly awash in a whole stream of brown and black and white. He could not remember other dogs, but he was delighted and kicked up his heels and wagged his tail. They ignored him and held to their course. When he got in their way, they snapped at him and kept going.

He was left alone again as suddenly as he had been surrounded. Why wouldn't they play with him?

Suddenly there was a clip-clopping and two horses rushed into view. He stared up in awe at the great beasts, and it took a while to realize that the upper parts of them were actually humans.

"Look!" said the Prince. "Look at those markings! That must be the pup that was lost from the litter of Crusher and Gwendolyn."

"Your Highness is right," agreed his Master-of-Hounds. "But he has been very ill fed and poorly groomed. Whoever kept him did not appreciate his abilities and his pedigree."

"Well," said the Prince, "we'll take him back with us and see if we can improve his condition and correct his training."

The Master-of-Hounds frowned. "Your Highness must not expect too much. Granted his blood lines are superb, but still the prime time for his training has passed. I doubt that I could ever make a true hunter out of him."

The Prince looked displeased. "That is no doubt true. Therefore I will handle his training myself." The Master-of-Hounds had more to say, but the Prince cut him short. "Fetch him!" he commanded, and wheeled his horse to follow the other dogs.

The Master-of-Hounds sighed and dismounted. Bilbo wagged his tail and frolicked in delight at this new friend. The Master-of-Hounds watched the dog's capering with disgust. He extended his hand in a gesture of command. "Come here!" Bilbo sat up proudly and held out his paw to shake.

It is amazing what a dog of breeding can learn to do if he has a good enough trainer, and the Prince was the best. Of course, the term "good" here has no sentimental moral overtones; it is used strictly in the sense of "skilled."

A good trainer is patient, steadfast, and unyielding. He pursues his end tirelessly, without regard for his own comfort or, naturally, that of the dog. He uses the whip without anger, when it is needed, and ceases without pity when the point has been made. He uses hunger as a fine tool, cutting away fat and laziness and shaping instincts into weapons. He uses pain as a language.

In a month, Bilbo learned to come when called by the name "Grinder." But he did not bark in reply to it and so was punished.

In two months, Bilbo learned to find a wounded bird brought down in the bush by an arrow. But he did not howl to lead the way and so was whipped.

In four months, Bilbo learned to bring the wounded bird back to his master's feet. But he did not whimper as he approached and so was beaten.

In six months, Bilbo learned to run with the pack. But he did not bay and so was cudgeled.

In a year, Bilbo learned to hamstring a boar, circling it

*with the pack and biting the tendon in its heel to incapacitate
it. But he did not growl to confuse the beast in battle and so
was driven away hungry while the others shared the prize.*

In two years, he learned to kill on command.

And he began to bark.

*It had been so hard for so long. The pain and the hunger
and the exhaustion. Many times he had wanted, had needed,
to speak, but the image of a young girl's tears had stilled his
voice through it all. Until the day his powerful jaws tore out
a deer's throat and the blood in his mouth sang to the blood in
his veins and he howled in the only triumph a slave can know.*

*"Good boy, Grinder!" called the Prince. "Now you're the
best."*

*There was food, there was rest, there was balm for his
wounds. It was so simple after all. Grinder needed nothing
more.*

Grinder he was now, and Grinder was the best.

"Now that's a good chapter!" Valorian enthused. "I
think that's the best you've ever written."

She looked at Teller with anger. "It's not meant
to be enjoyed. It's supposed to be ironic."

"Ironic?"

"You're not supposed to be happy that the dog
has changed."

Valorian looked doubtful. "Well, however you meant it, it's still a good chapter. Sometimes even the author doesn't know what she's really saying."

"Very true," she agreed, glaring at Teller. "Please go on. I think the end must be near."

Valorian looked around for something to drink, then decided he wouldn't want to drink anything in such a dirty place anyway and turned back to the pages.

On a lovely summer's day, the Prince went out with his pack to hunt. He was surprised to come across a lady struggling through the woods.

"Sir!" she cried, then saw the royal insignia on his saddle. "Your Highness!" She hesitated, then dropped a deep curtsy in the mud puddle she had been trying to cross. "Please help a poor woman in distress."

"Rise, lady," the Prince said, laughing to himself at her plight. She obviously thought she would have been punished if she had not curtsied at once, and she was right. "What can your Prince do for you?"

"It's my . . . serving girl. She's lazy, doesn't like the work, and now she's run away into the woods. I would let her go, but I'm concerned for her safety." The woman smiled, then frowned, then tried to look concerned. She finally settled for

curtsying again and trying to look like a very loyal subject.

He watched for a moment, enjoying her confusion. A mistreated servant was hardly a royal concern. Still, new sport was always welcome.

He moved his horse forward a few paces and pointed to the ground. "Are those her footprints?" When the woman nodded, he gave a shrill whistle. The dogs' heads whipped up toward him. He pointed to the prints and called, "Scent, boys!" They crowded around, nosing the ground. The younger ones bounded several steps along the path, then turned back, whining. The best of them caught the scent, then stood in silence to await the word.

"Hunt!" shouted the Prince, and a swirl of black and brown and white swept howling from the clearing. The horse tried to follow, but the Prince pulled him up a moment. "Her name?" he called.

"Etta," she stammered, dazed by the noise and movement. "Emberetta."

"Go home and wait," the Prince called. "You'll have your maid back." He reared his mount into a turn and lunged down the track.

It was glorious to dash through the trees, dodging low-hanging boughs, pulled along by the song of the pack in full cry. He could read their individual voices, hear their excitement as they closed on the prey. He could pick out Grinder in the lead. That was good. He would control the excitement of the younger dogs. This was not a hunt to the death, after all.

Her back was to a tree and her hands over her face when he arrived. The dogs stood in a circle, barking, snapping, twisting to look back at the Prince, wanting the word. In the middle of the circle stood Grinder, silent, staring, his coat twitching as if beset by flies.

"Easy, boy," said the Prince, springing down to stand beside him. He could feel the dog trembling against his leg. "Just a serving girl, nothing to get excited about. Well, girl, next time you'll do your work and not complain! Let's see your face!"

The girl slowly lowered her hands. The Prince was surprised. She was small, but obviously his own age. And she was beautiful. Pale and thin, but that only gave an otherworldly quality to her loveliness.

"It's all right, it's all right, don't be afraid," he said, soothing her as he would a dog. "I'm your Prince. Your mistress asked me to return you safely to her."

The girl stood straight and defiant. "My 'mistress'! You mean my stepmother. Although better for me if I had been her slave, because she would never have treated her property as badly as she did me! If you return me to her, I will die."

The Prince looked at her ragged clothes, at the marks on her arms and legs. And again at her face. He began to feel a movement deep inside to match the trembling of the dog beside him.

"Forget about her," he said. "How would you like to come to the Palace?"

"Any punishment you mete out would be welcome next to what she would do."

She looked so brave and hopeful, he had to laugh. "Not for punishment! I invite you to live at the Palace." She looked at him uncomprehendingly. "All the best of the kingdom is at the Palace. In my chambers, I have all the finest clothes and richest jewels of the kingdom. My stables hold the noblest horses, my kennels the fiercest dogs. You are beautiful. You belong in the Palace."

She could think of no answer and so she let her eyes sink. She found herself looking at a dog.

"Bilbo?" she said in disbelief.

Grinder took a step forward. "Get back!" the Prince commanded. The dog retreated a step.

"Don't be afraid," the Prince assured the girl. "He won't hurt you. He does only what I say."

"As I would have to do at the Palace?" she asked.

He smiled and shrugged, as if his absolute power of life and death left him quite helpless. "I'm your Prince," he said charmingly.

She knelt and he was pleased to think she was acknowledging his dominion. He was about to tell her to rise, when she extended a hand and said again, tentatively, "Bilbo."

Grinder was moving forward again. "Get back!" the Prince snapped. The dog did not stop. "Get back!" he repeated. Another step.

"Bilbo!" she cried with delight.

"His name is Grinder," the Prince snarled as he took the riding crop from his saddle and grabbed Grinder by the scruff of the neck. He yanked viciously at the loose skin there and raised the crop for a blow.

"No!" she cried.

With a howl of rage, Grinder twisted and threw his weight against the Prince. The other dogs scattered, yelping in confusion. The riding crop went flying. In an instant, the dog's powerful jaws encircled the neck of the prostrate Prince.

"No!" screamed Etta, scrambling forward on her knees, grabbing the dog's tail, his haunches, pulling herself up his body while the Prince felt wet teeth at his throat. The deep growl rumbled in his ears and hot breath filled his lungs. He was stunned. His life had always seemed to be the center of the universe, and now here it was reduced to a mere mouthful.

She tugged at the dog's ears. "No!" she screamed. "Don't do it!"

Grinder was confused. He sensed that the mere closing of his jaws would bring an end to all his pain. But there was something about this girl . . .

"Don't, Bilbo," she pleaded into his ear.

Grinder wagged his tail and lifted one paw to shake. But his jaws remained fixed and his growl did not waver.

"Please, Bilbo," she whispered, and her tears fell onto his face.

Grinder felt the tears. He knew that if he did not bite now, the pain would come back, worse than ever before. But he remembered something beyond all the pain and hunger and exhaustion. He remembered what love had taught him, and all his training fell away in a moment.

The growl dying in his throat, Bilbo turned and licked away Etta's tears in silence. She laughed and hugged him, and her heart was full.

The Prince stood slowly and dusted himself off. Shakily he remounted. He looked down in astonishment at the fragile girl rolling happily in the dirt with the great brute of a hound.

"Thanks for your help," he muttered. "Of course I shall have to destroy him. No dog of mine can behave that way."

She looked up at him. "Exactly. No dog of yours. He does not belong to you."

The Prince drew himself up. "You're not saying he belongs to you!"

She shook her head. "No. He belongs to himself. As do I. As do you. We can never truly own anything or anyone outside ourselves unless it is given freely. And then it is only ours if we give it freedom and freely it returns."

She turned and walked into the woods. Bilbo followed her.

The Prince thought of summoning his guards, of discipline, of punishment. But he suspected that she was right, that he would never own either of them, and he hated anything that was beautiful that he could not possess.

"Too bad you will never even see the Palace!" he called spitefully as they disappeared into the trees.

"Who needs a Palace when you have a friend? Right, Bilbo?"

She offered her hand to the dog, who obediently rolled over.

In later years, she often told him that it was all right to bark, but he never again made a sound. Out of choice, not training. As a gift to her.

"The End," Valorian read doubtfully. He looked on the back of the last page. "Where's the rest?"

"The rest?" asked Teller, avoiding the young woman's eyes.

"Yes, where she comes back and the Prince says something to make her feel better and they all live together happily ever so forth and so on. Don't they get a happy ending?"

"Some people would say that *is* a happy ending," Teller suggested.

"Not for the Prince. They don't end up together?"

"She had to make a choice," said Teller. He looked at her and she looked away.

Valorian scratched his head. "It's not much of a fairy tale, is it? I mean, there's no magic in it. And it's a little like some stories I've heard before, but not enough to make it amusing."

"I didn't write it," she said suddenly.

"I know," said Valorian. "You told me. *He* writes it, you dictate it to him."

"No!" she blurted, then blushed and went on. "I mean, I didn't make it up, either. It or any of the other stories. He wrote them all. He made them all up. I just told him the old versions. He did all the work. They're his stories."

Valorian looked back and forth between them for a moment, then laughed. "Well, thank goodness for that. I mean, fairy tales are fine when you're a little girl, but it's time to be outgrowing all that stuff."

"You don't mind?" she asked, and her voice held something of relief but something, too, of hurt.

"Tilly-Toiler," he said, "I'm delighted. I was afraid you were going to spend all your time in your chambers writing silly stories and I'd have to read them."

Teller's vague fears became crystal clear in that

moment. "Your chambers?"

"Yes," Valorian replied calmly, although the question had not been addressed to him. "In real life, people choose the Palace."

Teller ignored him. "I thought you were happy here."

"Happy, yes," she admitted, "but never satisfied. You had your words and your voices, but I was just telling stories and passing the time and waiting."

Teller gestured weakly at Valorian. "Waiting for this?"

"Waiting for something," she said.

"What can *he* give you?"

"Speak well of him, Teller. You don't have that many loyal readers."

"My reader, yes." Teller turned to him. "And what did you make of this story?" He gestured at the pages, which Valorian had tossed here and there as he finished with them. "What was its meaning?"

Valorian pursed his lips in thought; then he grinned. "Your bite should be worse than your bark?"

Teller was appalled. "Waiting for *this*?" he repeated to her.

"Oh, come now, old Plate," Valorian said cheerfully. "Must learn to take a joke. Let's see. How about, two unlikely creatures, or even people, can be happy as long as they are joined by love and willing to give of themselves to each other. There, didn't think I could do it, did you, you old dog?"

"No," Teller admitted. She looked as if she didn't expect it either.

"Which is an appropriate sentiment, since Tilly-Toiler and I don't have much in common, but we're going to be very happy together."

Teller went pale. "Are you all right?" she asked.

"Yes. It just hurts to be stabbed in the back with your own story. Well, Toiler, what are you going to do?"

She was suddenly crying, but her words were angry and bitter. "Don't call me that! Call me Toller, for I'm the bell that rings an end to things. Valorian has asked me to marry him."

"And you said . . ." Teller's whisper trailed off into silence.

She angrily dashed away the tears. "I have chosen the Palace."

"The Palace," Teller repeated.

"Yes, the Palace," Valorian chimed in heartily. "I'm seventh in line for the throne. I know that's not very close," he admitted with a frown, then smiled brightly. "But accidents happen! Anyway, I'll take good care of her. Or the household staff will, I should say."

"I have made arrangements," she said, businesslike, wiping at her eyes, "for the inn to bring your meals to you and do your washing and clean up now and then. If you need anything more, you may send a message. And . . . that's all. So good-bye."

Teller was nodding to himself. He spoke quietly. "Toller is well chosen. The knell has sounded."

"Nell Toller!" suggested Valorian with a laugh. "How's that for a name? Well, let's be going. Very pleasant meeting you, old man, or should I call you Bilbo? You should really try to learn some new tricks. Very nice stories and all. A bit trivial, but fine for children. That's it, then, so long."

Teller's last view of her was a pale glance back over the strong shoulder of Valorian as he led her firmly away.

Teller slowly gathered up the pages. He put them back in order and neatly squared the edges. It was the only original story he had ever written, and he had been very proud of it.

One sheet at a time, he carefully fed it into the fire.

Tale of
Tellers

She flung the door open with a crash. He looked up at her from his bed.

"What's all this about your not eating anything?" she demanded.

"It's good to see you again," he commented weakly. "Nice flowers."

She frowned as if she had just noticed the bouquet, and tossed it on his coverlet. "The innkeeper brought me the message that you send your meals away untouched. Did you tell him to tell me?"

"Nice dress," he said, reaching out to touch the

white lace of the bridal gown. "Is this what they wear at the Palace?"

She screwed up one side of her mouth. "Only at weddings. Which is where I'm supposed to be. Valorian will be upset that I'm late. Oh, he'll pretend it's amusing at first, laughing at his relatives' embarrassment and all that, but deep down he's no different and he'll be just as upset." She nodded to herself.

"I didn't feel like eating," he said, "after you left. I still don't feel well."

"Yes, but, I'm gone for good, so you'll have to get used to it. If you'll just eat, you'll feel better soon."

"Yes."

"Yes what?"

"Yes, I told the innkeeper to tell you. I wanted to see you one more time. I have an important question to ask you."

"And you'll eat now?"

Teller opened his mouth wide, like a baby bird.

"Well, I didn't bring anything with me," she said with exasperation. "I was going to a wedding, not a dinner party." Teller closed his mouth. She suddenly noticed how tiny he looked with the covers pulled up around his wrinkled face. "You're old," she said with surprise.

"I'll be better soon," he replied calmly.

"I mean you were always old. Now you're *really* old. I just noticed. I should hire someone to come and stay with you. An old woman or someone." She looked thoughtful. "I'll be rich now. I can do things like that."

Teller nodded.

She stood for a moment, fidgeting with the edge of her veil. "So if you're going to eat, then that's all settled." She gave a very definite nod of her head. "All right, then. Good-bye." She went out, closing the door quietly.

Teller waited, unmoving, watching the door. After a moment, it opened quietly, and she stared suspiciously from the threshold. "So what was the question and why was it so important?"

"It's good to see you again," he said.

"Don't start up on the dress again!" She walked angrily around the room, then stopped at the table, where fresh pens were neatly aligned next to a stack of paper. "Well, at least you've been writing. It's good to keep busy." But then she noticed there were no finished pages, only blank ones. "You haven't been writing."

He shrugged feebly. "No point with no one to read it. I lost my only reader." He paused and watched her closely. "I mean Valorian, of course."

"Of course," she repeated, then turned and stalked out through the doorway. "I forgot my flowers," she said when she returned.

"What if Sleeping Beauty didn't believe she'd been asleep?" he said.

She made a sound of disgust, grabbed her flowers, and slammed the door on the way out. She slammed it again on the way in.

"You see," Teller said, as if she had asked a question, "I was thinking about when a person wakes up. Do you know how long you've been asleep? Sometimes you think it was hours, and it was only minutes. And the other way around. How would you know you'd slept for a hundred years?"

She didn't want to think about it, but she couldn't stop herself. "A hundred years of wind and rain and storm would show, wouldn't it?"

"The forest of thorns covered and protected everything, and now it's melted away without a trace."

"Well, other people . . ."

"They were asleep, too."

"Other kingdoms . . ."

"*Rival* kingdoms, warring kingdoms—who would believe *their* stories?"

She was lost in thought a moment, then shook her head as if awakening. "All right, fine, so she doesn't believe she slept a hundred years. What difference does that make on my wedding day?"

He shrugged. "No difference to you or me. But imagine the poor Prince. Here he's performed a deed of great valor to win her, and now no one believes him."

That caught her interest. "And if he had a very high opinion of himself," she mused, "and thought everyone should admire him, and instead they don't even think he's a Prince . . ." She laughed out loud. "That would be even worse for him!"

He nodded. "Poor Prince."

"Yes," she agreed, reining in her laughter. "Is this a story you're working on?"

"No," he said, "I'm too tired to write. It's just a thought I had."

"Your voices."

He shrugged.

"Well," she said slowly, "I could make some notes

for you, if you like. The wedding can wait a few
more minutes."

She seated herself at the table, her back to him.
He smiled to see her there once more. She was
lovely in her gown, even if she did gather its folds
in bunches and shove them roughly out of the way.

"So what do I set down?"

"Start when the Prince defeats the evil fairy who
has turned into a dragon, and then he heads for the
turret room where the Sleeping Beauty lies."

"What are the words?" she prompted impatiently.

"I don't know," he answered weakly. "Just put
something down while I close my eyes for a moment."

She twisted around to look at him. "All right,
but then I'm going." She took up a pen and hesitated. "Fighting the dragon," she said definitely and
began to write. "Shall I read it to you?"

"No," he said softly, "just get the ideas down. I'll
read it later."

"Up the stairs . . ." she said. "He sees her. He
thinks it's a big romantic moment." She laughed.
"He kisses her. Big deal!"

"Good," he said. "Good."

As she wrote, she spoke more and more to herself. "She wakes up . . . looks around. Who is this?" She guffawed and slapped her hand on the table. "She asks for some identification! Ha! Take that, Princey!" She wrote faster and faster and spoke less and less. Sometimes she stopped to practice strange facial expressions, then dived back into it. "The dragon," she mumbled once, and "kitchen utensils."

Intent upon the hand that flew with the pen, she did not notice her other hand rubbing at her temple.

Teller watched as much as he could, smiling. She finally heard the voices. This was all he had ever wanted, to see her in his little room, carrying on his dreams. He made as little noise as possible when he died, so he wouldn't disturb her.

Her pen was racing and she was laughing and talking to herself as she neared the end, when the door opened again and Valorian strolled in. He made a point of being nonchalant, of not caring if he was noticed, but when he realized he wasn't noticed, he got very annoyed.

"I hope I'm not interrupting anything important, but there was a small question of a wedding, you may recall!"

She looked up, startled and guilty. "Oh! Of

course, you're right. I'm so sorry, it was just a final favor for poor old Teller here. I was taking down a story for him and I lost track of the time, and . . ." She stared at him, but her eyes went out of focus as if she heard something in another room and her hands went to her head. "Just a minute more!" she blurted, and ducked back to the page.

Valorian looked very cross at that, but he was determined not to let it show. At least the old man in the bed had the good sense to be quiet. Valorian waited patiently almost a full minute, but this writing was a boring business. He idly picked up the finished pages that were piled on the table. She started to protest, but she was too near the end and the words were crying to be penned, so she worked on while he read.

"All done!" she said finally, happily putting period to the last sentence. She beamed with satisfaction. "Oh," she said, noticing the ink blots that now covered the lacy sleeves of her gown. Then she noticed his frown as he read. She tried to take the pages casually from his hands. "It's nothing important," she said. "Just a story he wanted me to take down. A Sleeping Beauty story. Foolishness, really. We can go now. . . ."

Valorian looked at her accusingly. "This story is about me!"

She was startled. "What makes you think that?"

He pointed at a sentence. "'I am Prince Valorian,'" he read.

"Oh, yes," she said. "There is a certain similarity of names."

"Why did you put me in your story?"

"It wasn't me!" she insisted. "Tell him, Teller, it was all your doing." She turned toward the bed and gestured for the old man to confess. Teller was smiling and looking at the chair where she had been sitting. "Oh, he's too infuriating!" she exclaimed, stamping her foot. "He won't say anything when you want, but when you're looking for a little quiet, just try to shut him up! Let's go, it's not important."

Valorian pulled away from her and stepped toward the bed. Something was wrong. He touched the old man's hand. It was cold. He closed the unblinking eyes. "Come," he said, "we'll tell the innkeeper to take care of this."

She was staring, refusing to understand. "Take care of what? Why did you close his eyes? Teller, what's wrong with you?"

She stretched out a hand toward the old man, but Valorian took it in a grip both firm and gentle. "He's dead," Valorian said, turning her to face him. "It's time to go."

"He can't be dead. He told me the story. I wrote it down."

"He's dead."

A film of tears appeared in her eyes. "He can't leave me."

"You left him."

"That's different!" she snapped angrily, even as the tears slipped down her cheeks. "I could only leave him because he was here. You can't run away from something that's not there."

Valorian waited for something to make sense, but it didn't. He spoke quietly but insistently. "I know you think me unfeeling and unimaginative, but sometimes that's the best way to deal with things. Now is the time to get on with your life. You need to press forward and not look back. I know that's what I needed when *my* father died."

She drew back as if she would strike him. "He's not my father! He's just an old man I took care of. He meant nothing to me. It's just that . . ." Her voice broke and she trembled. "I was . . . *used* to him. Even if I didn't come to see him, I knew he was here." She stopped and pulled herself together with an effort. "Give us a moment alone. I have to finish something with the old man. Then I'll marry you."

Valorian suddenly saw her standing tall and beautiful in her ink-stained gown, with her long red hair and deep green eyes, filled with emotions he had read about but never really comprehended. He had often watched her in the way he watched his horses or dogs, proud of her bearing and grace or amused at her antics. Suddenly he saw her only as herself, a human being entirely complete and separate from himself. He felt a stab of fear. He had thought she belonged to him!

"Wait outside," she said quietly. "I'll be with you soon." Valorian nodded dumbly and started out. He hesitated, then picked up the rest of the story and took it with him.

She closed the door softly behind him and pressed her forehead against the rough wood grain for a moment. Then she turned and walked briskly to stand at the bedside.

She spoke firmly and precisely. "I just wanted you to know that I never stole again." She thought

a moment. "Except from you, of course. I could
never value what was given me, only what I took
for myself. And . . . I wanted to tell you that I read
your stories." She stood there looking down at him
for a while, then shrugged. "That's all. Just that I
read them. All of them. So you had two readers.
That's all. I read them."

"I know," said Teller.

Her eyes widened as she stared at the lips that
hadn't moved. "Did you . . ."

"I said 'I know,'" Teller repeated.

She waited for the shock, for the surprise to hit
her, but it never did. That surprised her. "So now
I've caught a case of the voices from you, have I?"

"When you were writing . . ." he prompted.

"Yes, I heard them. The Prince and the Princess
and the King and the dragon. They weren't so
much voices I heard, but when I tried to write
what I thought they should say, they kept surpris-
ing me and saying something else."

"Yes, you wanted the Prince to be just a fool, but
there was more to him than you expected and you
finally let him grow into himself. You finally liked
him."

"Characters can do that. I don't know if people

can." She looked toward the door.

"What drew you to your Valorian? No, don't tell me about wealth and power. You can try to fool yourself with that, but not me."

She thought hard. "He really liked your stories. He pretends now that he didn't, but he did. He didn't always understand them, but he liked them and I liked that in him. It gave me hope that someday . . ." She blushed. "Did you really know that I read your stories?"

"No. But I hoped you did. That was why I wrote them." There was a long pause, and she waited for him to ask hesitantly, "Did *you* . . . like them?"

"Like them?" she repeated. "How can you ask if I liked them?" She leaned close to his dead face to whisper with intensity. "I *hated* them! I *despised* them! They weren't proper stories at all! They wouldn't lie there on the page and be amusing—they'd keep rising up and talking straight at me! I'd bump into them when I was going about my business. All of a sudden they'd be there, full of questions, poking their noses into my affairs! What right had they to interfere in my life! Not proper stories at all!"

"They were the only way I could talk to you.

They tried to say all that I couldn't. Did you really hate them?"

She shrugged. "I suppose not. But they were like a bunch of people you have to spend all your time with, even though they get on your nerves and you can't figure out why you put up with them."

"It sounds like you're talking about old friends."

She nodded. "I guess that's true. You can't live with them, you can't live without them."

"I certainly can't," Teller said with a laugh.

"Ain't it my turn to palaver yet?" said a strangely accented voice.

"Not yet, Bill," said Teller. "You'll just have to wait your turn."

"Dagnab it!"

"Pecos Bill," Teller whispered. "He's impatient. Keeps cutting in line. You have to make allowances. He's from Texas."

She started to ask what Texas was, then stopped and touched her hand to her temple. "How many are in here? How many voices?"

Teller laughed. "A lot. And more all the time. You'd better get on with the writing, or we'll run out of cerebrum."

She pressed her eyes closed. "No! I'm not doing

any more writing. I don't want voices! This was an accident. I've got to get married and be rich. Valorian will never stand for it."

There was the sound of many voices crying "No!" and "Please!" Then there was a silence in her mind.

"You can stay, Teller," she said quickly. "I didn't mean you. I'm used to you. You can stay. I don't mind." The silence continued. She dropped to her knees by the bed. "Please, stay!" she begged into the silence.

She realized after a while that Valorian was standing over her. She wiped her eyes and stood, saying briskly, "Well, let's get it over with." She was out the door before she realized he wasn't following her. She stepped back in and said, "Well?"

He held the pages toward her. "Is this how you really see me? Arrogant? Vain? Rude?"

"It's just a story."

He looked terribly unhappy. "It makes me feel there's something wrong with me. It's not a proper story at all!" He didn't notice her startled expression at that, but hurried on. "A story is supposed to let me laugh at someone else, not feel bad about myself."

"We can discuss this later. Let's go get married now."

"No, I don't think I can marry you at all."

"What?"

"Not if you really feel like this." He held up the pages before her.

"Oh, don't be silly . . . Vally-Wally." She fluttered her eyelashes as she slipped into baby talk. "If 'oo is gonna be mean just 'cause o' silly old story, I is gonna stamp my foot." And she did.

He tried to look stern but couldn't. He laughed and hugged her, and she smiled back at him. "Well, Tilly-Toller, you know you're my favorite little girl!"

She pulled at his arm. "So, let's get mawwied!"

He laughed, but pulled away. "Just one thing first. Little girl has to prove that Vally-Wally is most important to her." He held the pages toward her. "Toss-um on the big bad fire."

She looked at the pages dully for a moment, then gave a giggle and a shrug. She grabbed them away and danced them over to the hearth. She blew on the embers and got a flame going and thrust the sheets of paper toward it.

She hesitated.

"Toss-um on, now," he chided from behind her. "Be a good girl."

She was staring at the words. At *her* words.

"Now, Tilly-Toller . . ."

"Teller!" she snapped.

"What about him?"

She spun to face Valorian. "Call me Teller!"

He was taken aback. "Why?"

"Because that's who I am." She straightened to stand before him.

"Are you going to burn it?"

"No," she said calmly.

"Why not?"

"Because these are my words. They're my heart and my soul. You might as well ask me to throw my*self* into the fire." His lip trembled and his face was full of hurt. She sighed in exasperation. "Don't you understand? This is my *voice*. It's made up of all the voices I have within me. And it would talk to you if you just opened up and listened." She touched his arm gently. "Do you ever hear voices?" she whispered.

Her eyes were wide and bright and there were things in them he couldn't bear to see, so he turned to look at the old man in the bed. "I envy you," he said. "You died happily." He gazed at the thin, smiling lips, and added softly, "Ever after."

"What?" she asked, not sure she had heard.

Valorian faced her. He had always been handsome, but now pain and acceptance added an unaccustomed strength of character to his face. "He died happily ever after. He won. You belong to him. You love him and you love writing. You're fulfilled by your voices. There's no room for me." He moved with dignity to the door. She watched in stunned silence.

"One thing I would ask," he said, his hand on the latch. "Send me whatever you write. I cannot promise to understand—that is not what I am good at. But whenever your voices speak, I will do my best to listen." He squared his shoulders. "Good-bye . . . Teller. I wish you joy."

"Valorian . . ."

He looked back, and in the very moment when he accepted the loss of what he had never possessed and realized the value of only in the losing, he saw the light in her eyes and felt her heart leap up with love for him for the first time. He could scarcely bear the joy of it and knew that given the chance, he would do something stupid.

He turned to the corner of the room and found himself facing the printing press. "Show me how this thing works," he commanded, blowing the dust off it.

"Why?"

"So I can set your story in print as you read it to me. That will be quickest, won't it? Then we can distribute copies of it . . ."

"At the wedding," she finished with a smile.

"Yes," he replied, looking at her, savoring the newfound pleasure of sharing, not owning. "At the wedding."

They shared a smile; then she gave quick instructions. "These letters fit in these grooves, and when we've got a page, we'll run it off. Ready now?" When he nodded, she began to read. "'Ducking under a gout of flame, the Prince threw himself forward into a double roll . . .'"

"Not so fast!" he pleaded. "This will take getting used to. What's a gout, anyway? Oh, well . . . g-o-w-t o-f f-l-a-m-e . . ."

She smiled and did not correct him. She would look it over later. There would be more errors.

"He'll do," said Teller in her mind.

"You're still here!" she thought happily.

"I'll be here as long as you remember me. This is how I live now, through you. And when you die, you'll pass on a bit of me along with some of yourself to whomever you have touched, to whoever has listened."

"More words, Teller," called Valorian. "Give me more words."

She read another sentence, answering to her name with pleasure and without surprise. It felt right and comfortable.

"You don't mind?" she asked him silently. "About the name?"

"I couldn't be more pleased," Teller replied.

Teller turned to look down at the face of the old man on the bed. He did look happy.

"There's hope for Valorian yet. It was a good turn of phrase, and quite true."

Soon to be married, soon to be buried, Teller regarded Teller and spoke together in one voice.

"He died happily ever after."